ROLL WITH IT

MELLANIE SZERETO

amatoria press

BOOKS BY MELLANIE SZERETO

Love on the Menu: Steamed Boxed Set

Nerds & Babies series ~

The Nerd Next Door

The Nerd Upstairs

The Nerd Downstairs

Nerds & Babies Collection

Nerd Love series ~

Comma Kaze

Comma Sutra (coming soon)

Romancing the Phone series ~

Call Me…Maybe

Smooth Operator

Hang-Ups (coming soon)

Telephone Lines (2025)

Dialed Up (2026)

Mixed Messages (2026)

The Jerk Series ~

Jerk in the Box

Jerk of All Trades

Small Town Jerk

Jerk the Ripper

Two Forks Hollow Christmas short story series ~

Snowballed

Two Nights Before Christmas

Mistletoe Miscalculation

CHAPTER ONE

BRENNA CARLSEN CLICKED ADD TO CART, NAVIGATED TO THE checkout, typed in her address and payment information, and pushed the Submit button before she lost her nerve. Then she saved a copy of the order confirmation on her desktop and second-guessed her decision to pay for expedited shipping.

"The only way to test your body's response to stimulation is to stimulate it. Buy a few different kinds of vibrators, and see what works and what doesn't."

Those words and that advice had come from her occupational therapist. The conversation with her dad's wife about sexual pleasure, orgasms, and masturbation had easily been one of the most embarrassing of her life, not that Christy had made it awkward. Helping people was her job, and she was damn good at it.

Next, Brenna opened the file on her screen labeled "Roll with the Changes." The name fit her life for the last eight years, four months, and four days—since the day she'd almost died. A document near the bottom of the list had been the only contents of the file until the first anniversary of the accident. She double-clicked on the name, ready to include a new item to the inventory of her intentions.

Goal #1: To not be a burden to my dad or my grand-parents.

Goal #2: To live as independently as possible in my own house or apartment.

Goal #3: To learn all I can about how to advocate for myself and others with disabilities.

Goal #4: To start my own architecture firm, focusing on new housing and renovation designs for people with disabilities.

Goal #5: To go on a date.

Numbers one and three were ongoing and always would be.

She'd accomplished the second after Christy had all but gifted her late father's house to Brenna shortly after they met. Instead of using the Claus for a Cause fundraiser money for the necessary remodeling project, she had suggested creating CAT—Creekside Accessibility Transport—for the disabled residents and senior citizens of Creekside. Not having to spend money on a down payment and not having a mortgage meant she'd been able to pay for accessible kitchen and bath counters and several other expenses herself.

Number four had happened three years ago, thanks to a grant. Accessibility In Mind Designs had grown from a one-person business to a seven-employee architectural firm since its inception, with an all-disabled staff—something practi-cally unheard of in the industry.

March's fix-up with a friend's husband's colleague counted as an accomplishment, even though the evening had been a complete disaster. Her date had arrived almost twenty minutes late, and he'd treated her like her disability was as much mental as physical. The only reason she hadn't left the loud, slow-talking fool before they ordered dinner was to cross Goal #5 off her list. Despite the bad experience, she wasn't giving up on having a social life that included a romantic relationship, marriage, and possibly children.

Setting her fingers on the keyboard, she typed another entry.

Goal #6: To find out if I can still enjoy sex.

Her spinal cord injury prevented her from walking, but the lack of sensation anywhere below her waist right after the accident had slowly evolved into regaining the ability to use the bathroom. Of course, the skill and strength required to move from her wheelchair to the toilet had taken months of training. Even now, the process was still a relatively slow one compared to a lot of people.

I'm luckier than most. No catheters or colostomy bags.

She saved the document, closed out of it, and prepared for her virtual meeting with the builder who was set to break ground on a residential neighborhood with several of her company's designs next month. It was her biggest contract to date and could prove to be a game-changer. New construction inhabited a whole different world from modifications to an existing home.

The ten-minute reminder popped up on her monitor as she reviewed the specs for the last of the eight floor plans she and her team had sold to her newest client. With the digital blueprints ready in the dock, she opened the email with the link, quadruple-checked the one o'clock start-time and took a small sip from the insulated bottle on her desk.

I'm a professional and can hold my own in a male-dominated industry. Be bold. Be confident. Be successful.

After another quick swallow of water, she clicked on the link and waited to be connected.

A few seconds later, her image with the background of

her home office appeared, along with a black rectangle with a name—Princess Zelda's Secret Uncle—in the corner.

A gamer is the owner of Hayes Builders? Well, that doesn't mesh with the phone calls and emails at all.

The screen name switched to Project Manager in the blink of an eye. Then, what seemed to be a chair creaking carried through the speakers and an annoyed voice joined the squeaky noise. He didn't sound anything like the friendly man she'd talked to before. "Knock on the door in fifteen minutes so I can cut this meeting as short as possible."

A barely audible response to his order came from the somewhere near the outer range of the microphone. "She isn't going to like that."

"Too bad."

Wonderful. I have to pretend he's not a jackass.

The black soul of Project Manager suddenly vanished to reveal rumpled brown hair, unreadable brown eyes, and a stern mouth atop a navy suitcoat and tie. "I'm overseeing the Creek's Edge project, so I'll be your new contact from here on out. Will that be a problem?"

Fighting to keep a neutral expression, she blinked instead of rolling her eyes. How many times did she have to put up with a bait and switch when contractors found out they were dealing with a woman?

She pasted on a fake smile. "No problem. Mr. Hayes seemed very excited to handle this himself. I hope he isn't sick."

Her nemesis's jaw ticked. "No, he's fine. Let's get down to business. I'm concerned about the width of the hallways. It means more subfloor, more underlayment, and more flooring, which adds to the cost of labor and supplies. I'd like you to modify all eight plans to have forty-inch halls instead of forty-eight. That's plenty wide enough for most furniture and appliances to fit through. And thirty inches is within the standard for doors, so thirt—"

"Have you ever watched a wheelchair-bound person try to navigate a hallway that's only forty inches wide? Not to mention trying to make turns into bedrooms and bathrooms with thirty-inch doors. AIM's specs are based on recommendations from the ADA and the medical community, in addition to the actual sizes of wheelchairs, walkers, braces, and other mobility devices. Something else to keep in mind. People with disabilities may also have a companion who assists them, either human or animal. At times, they'll need to fit side by side in a hall." Comfortable on her justified soapbox, she ignored his clenched jaw and the color creeping past the collar of his white dress shirt. "Creek's Edge is being marketed as a neighborhood with accessible homes. Your requests would mean Hayes Builders is misleading potential buyers and engaging in false advertising. Would you rather spend a little bit more on a product that performs as expected or have your company's reputation tainted by complaints? If necessary, I can arrange for you to see exactly how important these measurements are."

He lifted a coffee cup to his thinned lips, but she had no idea how he was going to swallow with his teeth grinding against each other like they were. The mug clunked when he lowered it, and a splash of dark-brown liquid landed on his shirt. He didn't seem to notice, which was probably a good thing, considering his nasty mood. "I don't have time for that."

Of course, you don't.

"Then I suggest you take me at my word. Accessibility is AIM's area of expertise. It's what we do every single day with every single client and project." She mentally crossed all her fingers and all her toes, because the ultimatum she was about to drop represented a line she would never cross. "And I won't compromise *my* company's reputation by agreeing to the changes you're asking for."

His scowl deepened, making his scrunched-up face look at least her father's age rather than the thirty-something she would've originally guessed. He obviously hadn't expected her to hold her ground. "I'm going to have to run the numbers again."

She gave a curt nod, but the small victory helped relieve some of the tension in her shoulders. "Unless you have any other issues with the designs or something else to discuss, I'll let you go. I wouldn't want to go over my fifteen-minute allotment."

His surprised expression turned sheepish, but it brought her no satisfaction. She still had to work with the ignorant ass.

He shifted in his seat and grimaced. "The secretary will be in touch to set up another meeting."

Before she could acknowledge his statement, he ended the video chat, testing her patience once again. "Better her than you, Mr. Project Manager."

CHAPTER TWO

LEANING BACK IN HIS UNCLE'S CHAIR, FLETCHER HAYES closed his eyes, hoping like hell the pain pill he'd taken kicked in soon. Given the choice, he would most definitely prefer a knee in the nuts to the pulled groin he'd gotten on the job two days ago. Now he was stuck in an office—in half a damn suit—for at least the next four weeks. Thank god for the basketball shorts he could hide under the desk. Uncle Nate had seized the opportunity to start training his successor, despite the fact that retirement was ten or more years out.

And my first thrown-in-the-deep-end assignment just had to be a meeting with the girl who didn't know I existed in high school.

Seeing her name pop up triggered more embarrassing high school memories than he could shake a sword at. Brenna Carlsen had been so far out of his league—valedictorian, cheerleader, class president, homecoming queen—and nice to everybody, despite being insanely popular. Now she ran a successful company and had a string of letters after her name, which meant she still outclassed him. Why would she want anything to do with a gamer who built houses for a living?

Especially after I pissed her off and killed any chance of that happening—if there was one to begin with.

A knock at the office door forced his eyes open. "Excuse me, Fletcher."

Right on time.

Too bad he'd forgotten to mute himself before admitting Brenna to the meeting, thereby sticking his foot in his mouth before he'd shoved it in farther. He used his right heel to spin toward the voice. "Thanks, Aunt Laura, but the meeting's over already."

"Oh. Hm." Her slight frown put him on edge as she crossed to him. "You look like you're in pain. Are you sure you're up to working today? Maybe you should go home and rest for another day."

He forced a half smile. Spending more time in bed or on the couch wouldn't make his muscles heal faster or his mood improve. It was worse than being confined to an office. "I'll be fine."

She brushed at a spot near his tie. "Looks like you spilled coffee on your shirt."

Of course, I did.

Not much in his life had gone as planned this week. Between the muscle strain and hearing about his ex-girl-friend's marriage and pregnancy, the past three days sucked enough without ruining his only white shirt and pissing off the architect for his uncle's newest endeavor.

He settled deeper into the chair, hoping to ease the pres-sure on his groin, but the change of position aggravated the soreness. "Do you know any tricks for getting out coffee stains? Something that doesn't require standing or hobbling around on crutches?"

"If you don't mind sitting around without a shirt on for a while, I can mix up a batch of dish soap, white vinegar, and water." Aunt Laura picked up his mug and set it on the stone coaster next to the landline phone. "That'll take it right out."

And make me smell like an Easter egg the rest of the day.

"Never mind. The painkiller barely took the edge off, so I'm just going to head home. Could you call Brenna Carlsen about touring one of AIM's houses? I need to see those hall and door widths for myself." He rolled backward to grab his crutches.

She patted his shoulder and then headed toward the reception area. "Wait here. I'll drive you after I make the call. Nate's still out at the jobsite."

Since he didn't really have a choice in the matter, he grunted a response and tried to breathe through the ache radiating from his abs to his knee. The doctor had asked him to rate his pain from stubbed toe to having a baby. How the hell did women survive childbirth if that was the worst on the scale?

The pain receded a fraction of an inch, and he froze to hold on to the feeling for as long as he could.

"Fletch?" Aunt Laura popped her head through the doorway. "Ms. Carlsen says she's available right now. Otherwise, it'll have to wait until the middle of next week. Are you up—"

"Let's just get it over with."

With a nod, she disappeared again for several minutes before her voice carried from the next room. "Stay put. I'm going to get my car. I'll be back in a jiffy to help you walk out."

Unlike the first time she'd offered, he kept his mouth shut. He had no doubt she could handle supporting all five feet ten and a half inches of him with her petite five-three frame. Small but mighty was the perfect description for her, and she could probably whoop his ass right now.

He struggled out of his jacket, tie, and dress shirt to swap them for one of the Hayes Builders long-sleeved t-shirts piled near the coffeemaker. They were probably for giveaways for marketing purposes, but the crews wore them on the job every day too.

By the time his aunt walked him outside and assisted him into the passenger side of a company SUV, exhaustion had joined the dull ache. He slumped into the seat and leaned against the headrest. "Sorry to need a chauffeur. I sure hope I'm back to driving next week."

"It's no trouble." She pulled away from the entrance and turned right onto the street when she was prompted by the slightly robotic voice from her navigation. "I'm going to run to the store for coffee and stop to fill my gas tank while you're doing your tour. Text me when you're finished."

"Okay. I appreciate it." Despite the temptation to close his eyes, he paid attention to the directions taking them to a newer neighborhood not far from the newly renovated library, two blocks of medical offices, and the small hospital. His uncle's company had built all the houses in this area before he'd moved back to town eighteen months ago.

She turned into the driveway of a sprawling brick ranch, shifted into Park, and helped him out of the car. "Text me when you're done."

Giving a nod, he positioned the crutches under his arms and hobbled up the ramp to ring the doorbell.

A disembodied voice that could be Brenna's spoke at the same time the lock sounded like it disengaged. "Please let yourself in. I'll be right there."

Not bothering to answer, he pushed down on the lever-style knob and maneuvered into a spacious foyer with minimal decorating. A light on the security panel to the left blinked when he closed the door behind him. The device was set about four feet up the wall instead of the usual eye level.

He continued several more crutch-steps into the space, pausing to check out the living room to the right. Movement at the other end of the wide hallway caught his eye.

A wheelchair rolled toward the foyer, the woman who refused to back down seated in it and her hands propelling her forward. She clearly wanted to demonstrate her points with a real-world application. As she stopped, her dark hair fluttered over her shoulder. Her eyebrows rose a fraction and she extended her hand. "Brenna Carlsen of AIM Designs. I'm glad you decided to take my advice."

Her curt tone assured him she hadn't been pleased with their virtual standoff, but he adjusted his balance to shake her hand. It was soft and warm in his, almost distracting him from his purpose.

He winced as he straightened and crossed his fingers the pain didn't worsen. "Fletcher Hayes of Hayes Builders. Please excuse the casual clothes. It's a lot easier to get around on crutches without a suit on."

"Sometimes comfort is more important than image." She glanced toward his throbbing groin. "If you don't mind my asking, what kind of injury do you have?"

"Pulled a muscle at work. Four to six weeks recovery time. I'd prefer four."

"Ouch." Her intense blue gaze went from determined to thoughtful in an instant. "I'm guessing you're ready to sit and rest for a while, so let's do an abbreviated tour. The kitchen is straight ahead. Why don't you lead the way?"

Although she'd parked the wheelchair close to the left-hand wall, he hesitated, not sure he could move past her without catching a crutch on the wheels or turning sideways. "I don't think I can get through."

A small smile curved her lips. "The hall is forty-eight inches wide. My chair is twenty-six inches wide. Just to give you a bit of perspective, some are wider. Since I'm not completely against the wall, that leaves almost twenty-two inches for you. And your crutches, of course. That should be plenty of room, don't you think?"

He sighed, knowing he'd lost the battle over hall widths. "You proved your point. Show me an interior door."

Rather than throwing an I-told-you-so smirk at him, she zipped her transportation in a half circle and wheeled away from him on the hardwood floor. "The half bath is this way."

His clunk-step, clunk-step pace was nowhere near as fast as her speed, but he finally caught up to her next to the laundry room. "This is a thirty-six-inch door, right?"

"Yes." She used her hands to wheel herself between the doorjambs and toward a toilet with metal rails on both sides. "I have roughly five inches on each side for my arms, which still can feel a little snug. A thirty-inch door won't work. Two inches on each side of the chair would injure my hands."

"You're right." Giving his arms a short break, he braced his shoulder on the trim and shifted all his weight to his right leg. "I apologize for my attitude. I was a jerk for questioning the measurements to save a few bucks here and there, especially when you obviously know what you're talking about. My only excuse is that I hate being stuck in the office. Well, and having a pulled groin."

A genuine-looking smile lit up her deep-blue eyes. "Apology accepted. The average person doesn't think about these things, either because they've never experienced being physically disabled or they don't know anyone who deals with inaccessible spaces on a day-to-day basis. You look like you need to take it easy for the rest of the day, so we can finish the tour another time if you'd like to."

He nodded and gestured for her to lead the way back down the hall. "Whenever it's convenient for you."

With a few quick pushes of her hands on the wheels, she exited the bathroom like an expert and zipped along the smooth floor. "I'll be out of town for a conference until Tuesday afternoon, but I should have time Wednesday morning."

"Sounds good. Name a time, and I'm here." Hopefully, he wouldn't have to rely on somebody else to drive him by then.

At the front door, she picked up a cell phone from her lap and tapped the screen as he hobbled across the foyer. "Nine fifteen? If that doesn't work, I have an opening at ten thirty."

When he reached the front door, he breathed through another twinge. "Nine fifteen isn't too early for the homeowner?"

"I'm the homeowner." Her relaxed expression morphed into something unreadable. She stared at him like she was waiting for him to make a judgmental comment. "And this is my wheelchair."

CHAPTER THREE

BED MADE.

Groceries and laundry put away.

Morning bathroom expedition done.

Brenna tried to answer the email on her monitor, but Fletcher Hayes' reaction a week ago played over in her mind for the hundredth time. Surprise had been the first emotion when she'd told him the house belonged to her. Astonishment had set in at the news that she hadn't used a wheelchair solely to demonstrate the need for the measurements he'd argued against. Pity hadn't followed—for a change. He'd simply thanked her for educating him and promised to have the Hayes Builders secretary confirm their next appointment by the end of the day.

Giving up on work for the moment, she opened the security app on her phone to check the garage camera. The live feed showed a navy pickup slowing on the street and making the turn into her driveway. Sunglasses hid the driver's eyes, but brown hair several shades lighter than hers and matching scruff announced her visitor's identity.

She pressed her hand to her belly to calm the butterflies that had decided to take flight.

Weird.

No guy had triggered a physical response of any kind since the accident—actually, well before then. She'd suffered through bouts of tummy tickles from a crush in high school. His face almost came into focus, but it dissipated before it could clear, like many of her foggy memories.

What was his name? Something with an M?

The doorbell ringing through the house chased away the name on the tip of her tongue and sent her heart thumping.

Breathe.

Using the menu on the screen, she navigated to the door lock and typed in the code. Then she moved to the intercom system on the wall. "Good morning, Fletcher. The door's unlocked. I'll meet you in the foyer."

As she wheeled down the hallway, the front door opened and he stepped inside. He still had crutches under his arms, but he seemed to put less weight on them than a week ago. His tentative smile kicked up the flutters that hadn't quite settled. "G'morning, Brenna. How was your conference?"

"Excellent. Everybody seemed to like my presentation. Christy's too. My occupational therapist. She's married to my dad. We did a lot of networking and met some really interesting people. I'm not super comfortable flying by myself, so it was nice to have a travel buddy." Snapping her mouth closed, she barely kept from rolling her eyes at her chatter. Since when did talking to a man spark angsty feelings and diarrhea of the mouth? "Would you like a cup of coffee or tea before we start the tour?"

"I'm glad it went well. Coffee sounds good." He waved her toward the kitchen and adjusted the crutches again. "Go ahead. You're lots faster than I am."

Glancing over her shoulder, she grinned and then moved along the hallway at a slow but steady roll. "Getting there is more important than being first. You're doing much better on the crutches. How's the pain level?"

His low chuckle reminded her that she hadn't yet experimented with the toys she'd ordered. "About a four or five out of ten most of the day, maybe? Worse than stitches. Not as bad as a broken bone. I slept for four hours straight last night and didn't cry like a baby when I put on real clothes this morning. Oh, and I can drive again."

"That's a definite improvement. Healing takes time." She veered to the counter to double-check that she'd added water to the Keurig after breakfast. "Regular, decaf, or hazelnut decaf?"

"Decaf please." He paused at the table, his gaze sweeping from one side of the room to the other. "Wow. This is really cool. I've heard about adjustable-height counters, but I haven't seen them installed before. The wall cabinets move up and down on tracks, don't they? Otherwise, you wouldn't be able to reach them."

She nodded and pressed the control to access the mug cupboard and waited for it to lower. "Pretty handy, isn't it? I went with top-of-the-line products, but they come in less-expensive versions too. That's what my layout specialist put in the specs for the Hayes Builders package. The bathrooms are outfitted with similar functionality. Anything in your coffee? I have oat milk and powdered creamer. And I think I've got some sugar and artificial sweetener packets."

"Black's fine." Instead of pulling out a chair, he moved along the U-shaped kitchen, studying every cabinet, appliance, and inch of countertop. "This workmanship is impressive. Did a Hayes crew do the install? Or did you use somebody recommended by the manufacturer?"

The machine slurped as it finished making his drink, forcing her to delay answering him. "The manufacturer sent out a rep to monitor and consult while Nate and two of his most experienced installers put everything in. That's when he got the idea to build a small community of accessible homes. About two years ago. He asked me then if I'd be interested in creating some exclusive designs for him once he found the right property. But you probably know all the details."

"Not really. He sort of threw me in the deep end when I got hurt last week. I've only been back in Creekside for a year and a half. He already had an eye on a few parcels, but I didn't know what for until last winter." He joined her by her makeshift coffee station and leaned against the counter.

Something about the way he stood, with his elbow resting on the polished quartz and his left foot casually crossed over his right, seemed vaguely familiar. "Wait. You said you've been *back* for a year and a half. You're from Creekside?"

He glanced away, but not before she caught his slight frown. "Yeah. I grew up here. Left when I was twenty-one and came back ten years later to work for my uncle."

"You graduated from high school about the same time I did." She wracked her brain for a clue to help her remember him and failed. "Some of my memories from before the accident are sketchy, so I have blank spots here and there. Not a lot. Just enough to be frustrating sometimes. Did we know each other?"

"I wouldn't say we knew each other, but we were in the same class. You hung out with a different crowd, so I'm not surprised you don't remember me. Plus, I went to the career center for construction my junior and senior years." A hint of pink crept up his tanned cheeks. "I wasn't exactly college material."

"Not everybody is. Besides, who would transform my

designs into actual buildings if we didn't have trade workers? Somebody has to build the foundation, frame the house, do the plumbing and electrical, hang drywall, and all the rest of it." Reining in the urge to continue trying to convince him he had no reason to be embarrassed, she swallowed the rest of her unsolicited speech. "Sorry for the soapbox moment. It's just that you should be proud of what you do. I certainly don't have the skill set to construct anything more complex than a cabin made from Lincoln Logs, but that doesn't mean I can't use a hammer."

His bark of laughter echoed through the kitchen and put a sparkle in his eyes, setting off the tingling sensation again. "My ego thanks you. When I told Uncle Nate I wasn't qualified to manage this project, he said the same thing. About the trades, not about Lincoln Logs. Is it okay if I ask about your accident? I know a guy who suffered a traumatic brain injury from a fall, but I doubt you've ever climbed around on a third-story roof, especially without a safety harness. Anyway, he has a lot of memory issues."

"I can't even imagine. That's a long way down." The image he created in her mind made her wince, but recalling her own nearly fatal event brought a wave of anxiety mixed with gratitude and undefined emotions. "I was in a car accident eight years ago. The other driver lost control of his truck when an undiagnosed brain aneurysm ruptured. He died at the scene, and I flatlined once in the ambulance and again on the operating table. Spinal cord injury. Internal bleeding. Severe concussion. I woke up three weeks later with no feeling from my waist down. I'm very lucky to be alive and luckier that the only major long-term issue is not being able to walk. The memory thing is mostly just inconvenient."

He paled as he stared at her, the stark truth of what had happened to her obviously catching him off guard. His mouth opened and closed several times before he finally spoke. "I don't know what to say. Sure, stuff like that happens, but... I'm glad you're okay. I mean, not okay, because you're stuck in a wheelchair. It's just... You're still alive, by some miracle, and that's pretty damn amazing."

She placed her hand over his on the padded grip. "Thank you. Most people avoid talking about anything remotely related to car accidents and being disabled when I'm in social situations. They're uncomfortable, like they can't have a normal conversation with me. Maybe it's because I almost died. Whatever the reason, I don't regret being in a wheelchair. I'm alive, and it's led me to do something I really love and be successful at it."

The color returned to his face, although he still watched her with a guarded expression. His hand shifted beneath hers and he gave her fingers a gentle squeeze. "That's an inspiring outlook."

Distracted by his callouses and how they might feel on other parts of her body, she shrugged. "I wish I remembered you."

He snorted. "This version of me is better. A little older, a little wiser, and not afraid to talk to you."

His honesty pleased her, even though she planned to search the bookshelf in the living room later for her high school yearbooks. A picture might jar something loose in her mind. "I hope we can talk often. You should drink your coffee before it gets cold. Or would you rather finish the tour?"

"I'd like that. More conversations with you." A tummy-tickling smile in place, he straightened, moving the crutches into place. "Coffee can wait. Let's do the tour so I can see what else I need to learn for this project."

She guided him through each room of her house, pointing out countless details that made living independently easier.

His unwavering attention to everything she showed him and said to him eased her concern about the finished housing—and the possibility that he might truly like her.

A quick scan of her bedroom assured her none of her lacy bras or practical underwear peeked out of the dresser as she wheeled into her private space. "The master bath and closet are through that door."

She parked near the cedar chest at the foot of her bed while he explored, waiting for his reaction to the accessible soaker tub, separate bench-seat shower, and the unique feature of her roll-in closet.

"Nice." His back was still visible in the bathroom doorway, but then he stepped into her favorite part of the house. After at least a full minute of silence, a familiar hum came from the closet. "Okay, this is too cool. I never would've thought to use the conveyor system of a dry cleaners to move clothes through the upper and lower racks. This is genius-level design."

Her lips curved upward in an involuntary grin from the compliment. "I don't know about genius. Maybe MacGyver level, since the technology already existed. I just put it to good use."

He barked a laugh. "If I'm ever stranded on a tropical island, I know who I want there with me."

Despite knowing his intended meaning, she couldn't stop her brain—and her body—from wishing the same. Heat surged to her cheeks, but it didn't slow the desire humming to life inside her.

She propelled her chair toward the window, hoping he wouldn't see the blush that was surely blooming across her face. Her elbow bumped the box on the cedar chest as she passed, sending it sailing to the floor. Its contents tumbled out and scattered beyond her immediate reach.

"Are you okay? Did you fall?" He rushed out of the closet as fast as his crutches allowed. The panic in his expression faded with a noisy exhale when he looked at her. Then his gaze dropped toward the still-packaged devices she'd ordered last week.

The embarrassment that had started to wane burned hotter, and she wanted to sink into the ground.

CHAPTER FOUR

"ARE YOU FEELING OKAY? WE CAN GO OVER THIS ORDER later if you need to rest for a bit."

Aunt Laura's voice jerked Fletcher out of the recurring daydream that had been on auto replay for the last five days. "Hm? Oh. I'm good. Just thinking about the, uh…"

Still reeling from discovering Brenna owned sex toys, his thoughts refused to cooperate with his mouth. Her whole face had turned a bright shade of pink when he'd picked up the trio of vibrators that had fallen out of the shipping box. Of course, he hadn't escaped without a considerable amount of heat creeping up his neck. She'd likely seen through his attempt to make up an excuse and leave before he asked if he could help her test out her new purchases.

That would've been weird, considering they didn't really know each other very well, hadn't gone out on a date, and had never even kissed. Besides, sex was out of the question until his groin healed—at least another two to three weeks.

He cleared his throat. "I have some questions about one of the places that makes accessible cabinets and countertops.

I'm thinking I should talk to Brenna Carlsen before we finalize the order."

His aunt's raised eyebrow and smirk said he didn't fool her. "Do you want me to find out if she's available for a lunch meeting? Or maybe you'd like to discuss it over dinner."

Was he that easy to read?

Grabbing his phone from the desk, he willed his insides to settle down. "I'll call her. We exchanged cell numbers the other day."

"Well, you'd better do it pretty quick. It's almost lunchtime."

Lunch or dinner invitation?

He shoved his fingers through his hair, completely thrown off-balance by how Brenna might perceive his interest in dating her after last week's mishap that had embarrassed them both. "Okay, I'll see if she's free for one or the other."

"I knew you liked her!" Aunt Laura clapped, spun on her heel, and hurried out to the reception area.

The door snicked closed behind her, leaving him alone with the worst case of nerves he'd experienced since high school.

Just call her.

A deep breath did little to calm his thudding pulse, but he pulled up his contacts, tapped on her number, and lifted his cell to his ear. With each successive ring, his hope shriveled a little more, until the beep for her voicemail forced him to choose between leaving a message or hanging up. "Uh... Hi, Brenna. It's Fletcher. I wanted to ask... I have some questions about the company that makes the cabinets. Can you give me a call when you have a few minutes? Or lunch. We could talk about it over lunch or dinner, if you don't already have plans. Or I'll try again later."

Could he have sounded any more like a desperate loser?

He set his phone face down next to the open laptop and cradled his head in his hands. Maybe he'd never been the greatest at talking to women, but the infatuation he hadn't grown out of had obviously inflated his un-coolness factor to a new level.

Letting out a frustrated groan, he leaned back in the chair. The motion stretched his obliques and sent a sharp stab through his sore muscles. He almost whacked his head on the desk as he doubled over in response to the pain. "Damn it, that hurts."

Rumbling vibrations pulled him from the pity party, but he forced himself to move slowly as he straightened. His hand shook as he reached for his cell, confirming his anxiety level was far beyond normal range. The name on the screen did nothing to ease the pounding in his chest.

Breathe.

He tapped the icon to answer and lifted the phone to his ear. "Hello?"

"Hi, Fletcher. It's Brenna. I got your message." Her hurried words put every cell in his body on high alert. "I have a lunch meeting today with my team, but dinner sounds great."

Relief washed away the itchiness crawling over every inch of his skin. "Great."

God, brain, you can do better than that.

He sucked in another calming breath and exhaled to the count of four. "I don't get out much, other than a beer with a few of the guys I work with once in a while. Where would you like to go? Do you have a favorite restaurant?"

"Well, I know pizza isn't very exciting, but I love Lorenzo's. Best breadsticks I've ever had." The enthusiasm in her voice conjured her gorgeous smiling face in his mind.

"I have to disagree. Pizza is definitely exciting, and excellent breadsticks are very important." He hesitated for a second, unsure whether she thought this invitation was turning into a date. "So, um, do you drive? I don't mind picking you up."

Her lengthy silence didn't seem like a good thing. "No, I don't drive anymore. I tried a couple years after the accident, but I froze. I just couldn't. The PTSD was too much."

Shit.

He wanted to kick himself for even asking the stupid question, but that would undoubtedly cause another stab of pain. Of course, she wouldn't want to drive after almost being killed in a car accident. Even being a passenger had to be stressful. "I'm sorry. I shouldn't have—"

"It's okay. I actually hate when people tiptoe around me, like I'm going to fall apart if they say the wrong thing. If it isn't out of your way, a ride would be awesome. Oh, but I'll need some help getting in and out of your truck, and you're still healing from your injury. I should make arrangements to have the transportation service pick me up instead."

Her suggestion sparked a wave of disappointment and a frantic grasp for some other alternative. "I, um... Hey, I can borrow my aunt and uncle's Crown Vic. The seats are probably about the same height as your wheelchair. That'll make it easier to move from one to the other, right?"

"Yes." She still sounded hesitant.

"And it has a huge trunk. Your chair folds mostly flat, doesn't it? It should fit, with room to spare. How much does it weigh?" He mentally crossed his fingers for a number that wouldn't keep him from lifting her chair.

"About thirty pounds. It has a carbon frame, so it's lighter than a lot of them, but should you be lifting anything with your injury?"

Glad to know they were on the same wavelength, he

finally let the tension seep out of his neck and shoulders. "The doctor said nothing over ten pounds during the first two weeks of rest and whatever's comfortable, within reason, after that. No bench-pressing a stack of two by fours. Today is two weeks."

"Okay. Are you sure your aunt and uncle won't mind lending you their car? Because I can make other arrangements if I need to." She seemed willing, even if she didn't want to inconvenience anyone.

"Hold on for a few seconds while I ask her." At her okay, he carefully rose and walked to the reception area, glad to finally be done with crutches. "Aunt Laura, is it all right if I borrow your car to take Brenna to dinner tonight?"

His aunt grinned up at him from her computer and mouthed the words no one appreciated. *"Told you so."* "Of course. Tell her I said hello."

"Thanks." He stuck out his tongue at her and then headed back into his temporary office. "Laura says hi and that I can borrow her car. What time should I pick you up?"

Faint clicking told him Brenna was typing away at her keyboard and probably getting ready to start her meeting. "Please tell her hello for me. Is five thirty too early? I usually work until five, unless I have a really big project deadline."

Feeling more hopeful than he had since returning to Creekside, he leaned against the desk and relished the agitation in his gut rather than cursing it. "I'll be done at five today too, so that's perfect."

"I need to go, but I'm looking forward to seeing you later."

The genuine-sounding enthusiasm in her voice boosted his mood and his confidence. "Same here. Have a good meeting. See you at five thirty."

"Thanks, Fletcher. Bye."

As he set down his phone, his heart did some sort of swoopy thing, like it had every time he'd seen her in high school. No one else had ever inspired that kind of reaction, not even the girlfriend he'd dated for over a year. The breakup and her recent marriage to his former co-worker made sense now. The missing spark had always been meant for different people, not them.

The next five hours passed slower than any in his entire life, giving him plenty of time to think and rethink his plan for his maybe-date and saying goodnight. What if he leaned in to kiss Brenna and she demanded to know what the hell he was doing? Should he ask her for permission?

Aunt Laura knocked on the open office door and jingled a set of keys, jerking him from his daydream about a first kiss. "Victoria is parked out front. I took her through the car wash and she has a full tank of gas. We'll swap vehicles back tomorrow morning. Now, get out of here and have a wonderful time on your date tonight."

He tried and failed to stop a grin from divulging his excitement as he stood. "Thanks again for the loaner. I promise to be super careful with your baby."

"You're welcome." She wrapped her arm around his waist and squeezed when he escorted her back to the reception area. "All teasing aside, I really hope this works out. It's obvious how much you like her."

If his aunt could read his feelings, would Brenna be able to see them?

Keys in hand, he huffed out a noisy breath. "Do you think she likes daisies? I thought I'd stop at Dottie's Floral Shop on the way home. You know, as a thank you for being patient with my ignorance about the hall and door measurements."

"Or maybe because you want to impress her with flowers?" She gave him a gentle push toward the exit. "Either way, daisies are a good choice. Simple but sweet. Now, skedaddle already. You don't want to be late."

"Yes, ma'am." He lumbered outside with her brassy laughter chasing him all the way.

At twenty-six minutes after five, he eased out of his aunt's car with a bouquet in hand and tried to calm his nerves on the walk to the front door. His nicest pair of jeans, a short-sleeved button-down shirt, and newish hiking boots were acceptable for a pizza date, weren't they?

If this is a date.

As he raised his free hand to push the bell, the door swung open.

Brenna's welcoming expression, bright blue eyes, and formfitting summery dress took his breath away. She glanced toward the flowers and her smile widened. "Hi, Fletcher. Do you want to come in for a minute. I just need to grab my purse and a sweater."

"These are for you." He held out the bouquet and stepped inside when she maneuvered her chair back. His stomach churned at the prospect of telling her his true intentions, but it seemed like the right thing to do. "I appreciate that you took the time to help me understand how important it is to stick to your designs. And, well, I'm hoping we can make this a date. I like you, and I, um…"

Her frown didn't bode well. "I like you too, but I also don't want to put our work relationship at risk. Or either of our careers. What if we go out as friends for now? Just until any changes are finalized and the project is underway. And then we can decide if we're still interested in being more than friends."

CHAPTER FIVE

"DAD, YOU REALLY DON'T HAVE TO DO THAT TODAY. DON'T you have jobs lined up to replace missing shingles for paying customers?" Brenna wheeled after her father as he walked out of the kitchen.

He grinned at her over his shoulder, but he didn't slow his pace. "You paid me with coffee and breakfast. Besides, Christy mentioned she wanted to talk to you about something important this morning. I'm guessing occupational therapy stuff. Or what you want for your birthday. I'll be done in about twenty minutes."

Knowing full well she'd gotten the stubborn gene from him, she made a quick U-turn in the foyer. If he wanted to sacrifice twenty minutes to do a quick repair on her roof, who was she to argue?

"He loves taking care of you." The words her not-quite stepmom spoke were the truth. He'd chosen to dedicate his life to being the best dad he could be since his ex-girlfriend had given birth and signed away her parental rights almost thirty-three years ago.

Brenna rolled up to the table where Christy sat with a cup of tea. "I know, and I love giving him a hard time about it."

Christy barked a laugh. "Understatement—for both of you. I would've given anything to have that kind of parental bond when I was growing up."

"You deserved better, but we don't always get what we think we've earned, do we? Although, you and Dad eventually got your happily-ever-after. Or, at least, the closest thing to it."

Lifting her mug from the table, Christy nodded with a dreamy smile. "You're right. Speaking of deserving, I was wondering how you're doing with your latest goal. Did you find any interesting vibrators to order? Tell me about your progress."

A cold sweat broke out on Brenna's shoulders and neck, but she willed it away. Frank discussions about body functions were a part of her reality. "I ordered three, but I haven't tried them yet. At first, I was nervous, which I know is normal. It's just that... When Fletcher Hayes came over for a tour of the house last week, I knocked over the box and they fell on the floor at his feet. I've never been so embarrassed in my life. They were still in their sealed packages, but, geez. He turned fifteen shades of red and acted like he couldn't leave fast enough. Then he asked me about dating when we were going out to dinner to talk about accessible cabinetry on Monday. I told him I thought we should just be friends while we're working together on the Creek's Edge project. I like him and he seems nice, but I don't know if he's being sincere or thinking I'll sleep with him because of the toys. Or maybe I'm some kind of novelty or something. Have sex with the crippled girl to see what it's like. Damn it, I hate feeling insecure about this."

The woman who'd helped her learn how to free her

wheelchair from a pothole eight years ago leaned forward and looked her in the eye. "You're an amazingly smart, strong, and generous person. It's okay to question other people's motives and doubt yourself once in a while. We all do. It's hard to be confident one hundred percent of the time. So, let's focus on you first. Ordinarily, I'd say give yourself some grace, but I think you need the answers to the foremost questions in your mind. Can I be sexually aroused? Can I experience an orgasm? What does it take for me to have an orgasm? Start there. If it doesn't happen right away, try again. Be patient with yourself and your body, and order more vibrators if this batch doesn't get the job done. Your pleasure is about you and no one else right now. You know what else? If Fletcher's only interested in sex, he'll get bored long before you're ready to jump his bones. It's no reflection on you."

Grateful for the billionth time that Christy had decided to stay in Creekside, Brenna pulled her into a hug. "I love that you don't pull any punches or let me feel sorry for myself."

"Not in my job description." Christy squeezed her a little tighter. "As soon as your dad's done on the roof, we'll get out of here so you can have some privacy. There's no physical reason you can't do this and enjoy it. Remember that fact when you get frustrated, because I'm guessing it isn't going to be as easy as you think it should be. Call me if you need to vent."

Brenna gave a curt nod. "So, basically, you're telling the perfectionist not to expect perfect."

One of Christy's eyebrows rose. "Has sex ever been perfect for you? Like blow-your-mind spectacular? Maybe start with your expectations as low as your least-satisfying sexual encounter. That includes manual, oral, vaginal, and any other experiences you've had."

"Ha! Good, sure, but not great." One memory stood out

among her modest history. Even including non-intercourse play, she could count the number of men who'd touched her on two fingers. "The guy I dated right after college thought I orgasmed every time I made a noise. Nice guy. Totally clueless about sex."

"Oh my god. That's pretty bad. I'm thinking you should start out a step up from that." Christy drained her mug and carried it to the sink. "You'll figure this out, just like you have everything else."

The front door clunked shut and three footsteps carried from the foyer. "The torn shingles from last month's storm are fixed. Am I allowed back in the house?"

At her almost-mom's questioning glance, Brenna resigned herself to the possibility of failure. "Yep. Thanks, Dad."

"You're welcome, Bee." He appeared in the doorway and his gaze went straight toward his wife. The look of adoration he aimed at her sparked a twinge of envy. "Ready to go, Mrs. Claus?"

Christy breathed a swoony sigh, clearly remembering their Santa-themed wedding in the park after the Claus for a Cause fundraiser soon after her return to Creekside. "Whenever you are, Mr. Claus."

Hiding her ridiculous feelings, Brenna pretended to gag. "You two are sickening sweet. Get out of here so I can tackle my to-do list—unless, of course, you want to finish my laundry and feed my handy little robot-sweeper."

He chuckled and crossed to her. His hug warmed her from the inside out and stayed with her as he straightened. "As fun as it sounds, I'd rather not tangle with your shoestring eater. Once was enough. Are we still on for grilling tomorrow?"

"Absolutely. Your Father's Day present needs to see some action." Too late, her words registered. His new grill had likely seen far more action since she'd had it delivered to him two weeks ago than she had in nearly a decade. "I'm bringing peanut butter cookies."

"My favorite. I heard there's a bingo tournament at the community center tomorrow. Do you want me to pick you up instead of trying to book a ride on the CAT?" He slipped his hand around Christy's as she stood.

Once again, Brenna shoved the sting of disappointment deep into the imaginary box of what-might-never-be. "That's probably a good idea. Text me when you're getting ready to leave, and I'll meet you outside. Thanks again for fixing the shingles. Love you. See you tomorrow."

Taking the hint, Christy tugged him down the hall. "Have a productive rest of your day."

The front door clicked shut several seconds later, leaving her alone with her persistent doubts. "I'll settle for one mediocre almost-there orgasm."

After a quick cleanup of the kitchen, she moseyed her way to the master bedroom's closet, where she'd stowed the source of her indecision. The box seemed to mock her from its place on the shelf. Despite the accident that had taken her ability to walk, most of her life had been relatively easy— school, sports, dating, being able to use the bathroom. Her gut said sex would be the exception.

"Screw it all." Snorting at the accidental pun, she grabbed the box and carried it to her bed.

As she lined up the three devices, the small text on the front of each package caught her eye. The U-shaped and G-spot vibrators needed a charge before use, and how had she not noticed the clitoral stimulator required triple-A batteries?

The latter would have to wait until her next grocery delivery since one of the TV remotes had eaten the last of her meager supply. She couldn't exactly hop in the car and drive to the store. Instead, she opened the other two toys and plugged them into the USB outlet mounted to the wall by her nightstand. When they were ready in a few hours, she would dedicate her afternoon or evening to testing them—and herself.

Or I can quit behaving like a wimp about this and use my fingers.

Moving from her chair to the bed took almost no time with all the practice she'd had. Thankful she'd chosen to wear a sundress, she leaned against the pillows and went to work on the row of buttons from her breasts to her knees. Then only her shapewear shorts remained between her and possible pleasure.

And my brain.

As she freed her second ankle and tossed the ball of pink nylon and elastic toward the far side of the mattress, the doorbell rang. She dropped her head back against the pillow. "I'm not answering that."

A knock followed several breathless moments later.

No way could she reach the intercom on the wall in time, and checking the video feed wasn't an option since her phone was still tucked in the side pocket of her chair.

Another knock carried from the foyer. "Brenna? Are you here?"

Her heart paused for a beat before her pulse hit panic mode. What was Fletcher doing here?

"Brenna, are you okay? I just talked to your dad at the hardware store and he said you were home." His voice was louder, like he was walking down the hall. The faint squeak of rubber soles against hardwood warned her he was getting closer.

She tugged the edges of her dress together and tried to fasten the top button. It slipped free, forcing her to start over.

Fuck, fuck, fuck!

"The door was unlocked, which is really weird. Are you hurt? I'm getting really worried. Brenna, can you hear me?" His urgent tone triggered a wave of guilt.

Should she answer him?

While she was still fumbling with the third button, he stepped into her bedroom. His eyes met hers and widened as they skipped toward the vibrators charging on her nightstand. He whirled around, turning his back to her. "Shit! I'm sorry. I didn't mean to... God, I'm so sorry. I thought something happened to you."

The floral-print cotton folded and gaped open, telling her she'd missed a hole, not that it mattered when the remaining dozen or so buttons weren't fastened at all. Embarrassment collided with a ball of frustration too wieldy to handle. Tears welled and spilled onto her cheeks before she could fight back, and an unexpected wail escaped.

She rolled away from him, using her momentum to drag her useless legs with her. Why couldn't she curl into a ball and wallow in self-pity like a normal person?

The mattress dipped and arms closed around her, cradling her to a solid chest. He wrapped her in a cocoon without pawing her nearly bare breasts, barer ass, or long-neglected vaginal region. "I mean it, Brenna. I'm really sorry. This is all my fault. I shouldn't have let myself in, but I... I just shouldn't have."

His breathy words on her ear and neck heated her skin, but his willingness to shoulder the blame for catching her during her first masturbation session in years warmed far more than her nerve endings. The attraction she'd been trying to rein in since their discussion about dating swelled. She wanted more than friendship from him, even if it meant risking their professional relationship. She also wanted more than sex, even though it meant risking her heart.

Half a dozen slow inhales and exhales finally let her relax her muscles and gain control of her wayward emotions. "I was preoccupied when my dad and Christy left and forgot to reset the security system. They would've freaked out and come in too. That would've been just as humiliating."

"Why? It's your body. You're allowed to touch yourself if you want to." He huffed out a humorless laugh. "The truth? I'd be doing it on a fairly regular basis if I could, especially lately. This woman I really like is off-limits for the time being. And I'd like to take things kind of slow if we start dating, but my dick hasn't gotten the message. Walking around with a hard-on all the time isn't very comfortable, so giving it part of what it wants would be a nice option."

An involuntary smile slipped along her lips and then faded when reality kicked in. Considering he'd already seen her naked and about to play with her clit, being completely honest with him didn't seem like it could be any more embarrassing. "I haven't touched myself or been touched by anyone else since the accident. The doctors say there's nothing wrong down there, but I haven't tested it. What if I can't feel all the things anymore?"

CHAPTER SIX

BRENNA'S QUIET ADMISSION OVERRODE EVERY THOUGHT IN Fletcher's mind, even the vision of her mostly nude body. He wanted to offer his help, but doing so would probably come across as creepy as fuck. Besides, she didn't need him to solve her problems for her. She was perfectly capable. Hell, she was more than capable of doing anything she set her mind to.

Careful not to cop a feel, he tightened his hold on her and kissed her temple. "You're one of the strongest people I've ever known. If it doesn't work the first time, you'll try again."

"That's the problem. My brain won't shut off enough to let me focus on a first try." She sighed against his forearm, perking up his attentive dick even more. "My fatal flaw is that I'm a perfectionist. If I fail at this, I also fail at the chance to get married. What guy wants a wife—or girlfriend, for that matter—who just lays there like a blow-up doll during sex?"

Before he could temper his response, he shifted so she

was on her back and he was looking down at her. "I know I agreed to be friends for now, but I need to prove something to you. Is it okay if I kiss you? For real. The way I really want to."

Her breath hitched, but she nodded and licked her lips, tempting him to dive right in.

Instead, he cupped her jaw in his palm and brushed his mouth against hers once, twice, three times in a barely there caress. Fire raced through his body at the contact, igniting every nerve ending. Still, he savored the light touches. They also gave her the opportunity to tell him no or ask him to stop.

The world fell away as he continued to kiss her. He pressed his lips to hers with a little more pressure and rubbed his thumb over the silky softness of her cheek, enjoying every second of being able to experience this with her. The need to show her how much he wanted her outweighed the urge to tangle their tongues together. He wanted an emotional connection with her as much as a physical one, both of which would require patience if he expected it to last.

That said, he'd already waited almost half his life to be welcomed into her inner circle. Considering how vulnerable she'd been to share her most private concerns with him, he could only assume she trusted him on a level far beyond that of anyone else, except maybe her family.

When he trailed kisses to her chin and then in a slow path to her ear, she combed her fingers through his hair and whimpered. "What are you trying to prove? That I can feel desire? Because I do. I want you to kiss and touch me everywhere."

"No, although I'm glad you feel those things." He nibbled on her ear lobe to distract his burgeoning dick. "The point is that I care about more than sexual positions. I really like kissing you and making you feel turned on. Would I love for you to come? Sure, but my job is to try to give you as much pleasure as your body is capable of. You'll never disappoint me. Showing you that you matter to me is the goal."

Her hand moved down his chest, amplifying the tightness in his jeans. "Since it's your job to make me feel good, you should—"

He dropped his lips to hers again for a final kiss before rolling to the edge of the bed. Standing took a bit of effort between his rock-hard erection, a still-healing groin, and the woman staring up at him with seduction in her eyes. "I have only so much willpower, you know."

Her lips turned downward into a sexy pout, inviting him to abandon his good intentions. "You're going to leave me all hot and bothered? That hardly seems fair."

Taking a step back, he shook his head to regain enough self-control to go home. "For what it's worth, I'm hot and bothered too. You're ready to touch yourself, like before I interrupted. No pressure to perform for me or anyone else."

"But…" The pure desperation on her face nearly pulled him back onto the bed with her.

"Once we've gone out on an actual date or two, we'll talk about swapping orgasms." He fished his keys from his pocket and shuffled backward toward the hall.

"First date. Tonight. There's a concert in the park. Pick me up at five." She cupped her breasts and brushed her thumbs over her nipples. They puckered into tight buds he wanted to taste. "If you bring supper, I'll provide dessert."

A groan snuck out and his dick twitched. He swallowed to keep from drooling. "Five o'clock. Right now, I need to go home and take a cold shower."

"Or you could think about me and handle your problem another way. I'll be thinking of you." She ran her tongue along her lip as she plucked at her nipples again. "We can discuss the results later. Drive safely."

"Always." He blew her a kiss and forced his legs to carry him out of the bedroom. "I'll lock up and reset the alarm on my way out."

Saturday traffic on the drive home kept him from indulging in fantasies about Brenna pretending he was there with her while she masturbated. God, he could spend hours worshipping her, kissing her, caressing her.

Got to slow down.

No woman had ever knocked him so far off-kilter like Brenna did. He could easily fall in love with her. Hell, he'd already jumped.

He headed straight for the bathroom, kicking off his shoes and stripping off his clothes as he passed through the bedroom doorway. A cold shower wasn't the solution, so he turned the water to hot and walked into the tiled space. The spray pelted his skin as he soaped his hand and wrapped it around his cock.

She appeared in his mind, sprawled out on the blue comforter that was a few shades darker than her eyes. Her pale skin practically glowed against the deep color, and her nearly black hair fanned out on the pillow.

He stroked up and down in time with the glide and flutters of her fingers over her clit and her rosy nipples. Her lips parted on a needy moan, driving him to pick up his rhythm and cradle his balls.

Their rough breathing and heartbeats synced as her eyes widened. Then a look of utter euphoria joined uninhibited cries and the trembling of her body when she shattered.

Everything inside him exploded at the beautiful image. "God, Brenna. Yes. Fuck, yes."

His lower abs and inner thigh protested against the sudden tense-and-release action in his muscles, causing a jab of pain.

Grabbing for the wall, he sat down on the built-in seat and tried to catch his breath. Bending forward eased the worst of the residual ache, but he had to squeeze his eyes shut to stop the pitch and sway of the floor. "Damn it, damn it, damn it. Okay, so sex is definitely out for another week at least."

When the disorientation passed, he slowly rose to turn off the water and dragged the towel over his wet skin and hair.

Damn, I hope Brenna's orgasm worked out better than mine.

After he downed an ibuprofen, rounded up his clothes, and dressed, he curled up on the couch with a bag of frozen corn and his phone. A picnic supper was his responsibility for tonight's date, but his refrigerator needed restocking and his cooking skills were mostly limited to grilling, making spaghetti, and pouring cereal into a bowl. They'd shared a pizza at Lorenzo's on Monday, and Italian and Mexican were kind of eat-at-a-table meals. Something simple he could stow in the cooler with bottled waters would be the best option.

"Maybe…" He navigated to the messaging app to fire off a text to Aunt Laura. *"Does the grocery store sell those charcoal tire boards? Like already made?"*

Less than a minute passed before dots appeared in the bubble. *"What the heck are charcoal tire boards???"*

"Stupid autocorrect." He typed in the letters again, checking to be sure his phone didn't substitute nonsense for his atrocious spelling this time. *"Charcuterie board. I think? The tray with cheese and crackers and stuff."*

"LOL That sounds much more appetizing. Yes, that's what it's called. They're in a refrigerated case between the produce section and the deli counter. How are you feeling today? Do you need me to bring over some heat-and-eat meals?"

Admitting he was currently icing a sore spot would trigger her motherly instincts and lead to questions he really didn't want to answer, like how he'd managed to overexert himself on a day off. *"Doing okay. I need to pick up some picnic supplies for later."*

"Ooh, a picnic! Do you have a date with Brenna?"

He snorted at the line of crossed-fingers emojis that immediately followed. *"Yes."*

"Yay!!! I want to be nosy, but I'll refrain. Have fun! Love you, Fletch."

His decision to move back to Creekside validated once more, he sent her a pink heart. *"Love you too. Thanks for the assist."*

"You're welcome!"

He tapped on the grocery store app, hoping he could find what he was looking for and swing by on the drive later. After several searches and additions to his list, he was satisfied with his choices and calculated when he needed to leave to arrive at Brenna's house no later than five.

As he shifted to get more comfortable, an important fact occurred to him. *"Aunt Laura, is it okay if I borrow your car again? I don't want to make riding with me difficult for Brenna."*

No way, no how would he be able to help her into his truck with today's setback. She probably wouldn't appreciate having to depend on him to get in and out anyway.

"On my way. Be there in a few minutes with some of Nate's oatmeal scotchies."

He responded with a drooling emoji. Contrary to his date's intimation, cookies and some kisses promised to be the only desserts they'd get to enjoy tonight. Between the pain reliever and the bag of corn doing their job, his muscles had settled into a mild ache, but any action would have to be one-sided.

Not that I'd mind.

She might, though, and he wasn't about to commandeer the discovery of what her body could and couldn't do. He admired her determination and independence—her strength.

After returning his makeshift icepack to the freezer and collecting the keys and scotchies from his aunt, he retreated to the game room and settled in for a quest with Princess Zelda. If nothing else, it would keep his mind off what Brenna was up to.

His stomach grumbled sometime later, but he didn't bother to check the clock. All his focus was on avoiding the lava flows blocking his path as he trekked toward the temple. Vibrations zinging through his hip jerked him from deep immersion in the game, causing his thumbs to slip on the controller and make him jump into the river of molten rock to his left. The screen faded to darkness, the death knoll of Link until he respawned.

Pausing the game, Fletcher fished his phone from his pocket. Brenna's name appeared, along with three overlapping text bubbles.

"I need to cancel."

"I know it's last minute."

"I'm sorry."

A handful of scenarios rushed through his brain, all of them bad. With his heart pounding, he pulled up her number to call. Each unanswered ring amplified his panic.

He pushed to his feet, ready to find his shoes when she finally picked up.

"Hi." Her tentative greeting sounded nothing like the confident woman he'd gotten to know.

"Hey. Are you okay? You're not sick or hurt, are you?"

Surrendering to the burning need to see her, he hurried next door to his bedroom to slip on a pair of trainers and grab his wallet.

"No, just feeling broken." The defeat in her voice cracked open his soul.

"I'm coming over. We can stay in and order delivery if you want." The Crown Vic keys in hand, he ignored the flopping laces of his untied shoes as he hurried outside to the car parked in front of his garage. "What happened?"

"More like, what didn't happen. Fletcher, I really think you should find someone else to date. I mean it. I'm still too much of a work-in-progress."

Her words stopped him in his tracks, half in the driver's seat and half hanging into the driveway. "What didn't happen? Oh. *Oh.* No, I'm not dating somebody else. I like *you.* And…and…I'm at least as much of a work-in-progress as you are."

"But, Fletcher—"

"No, Brenna." He moved his leg into the car, yanked the door closed, and started the engine. Hoping the short drive to her house would give him time to convince her, he switched to speaker so he had both hands on the wheel. "If anything, you're too good for me. Not the other way around. You're smarter and kinder and prettier."

She choked out a laugh and then sniffled. "Stop it. You know how to build houses and you're one of the sweetest guys I've ever met. And I happen to think you're very handsome."

"I'm the sweetest, huh? Then why are you trying to get rid of me?" She was silent as he turned onto Main Street. "Nobody's perfect. God knows I'm not, and I certainly don't expect you to be. We could be imperfect together. I don't know about you, but that would make me deliriously happy.

You and me. Nice and sweet, like apple pie and ice cream. Or grilled cheese and tomato soup."

"You make a persuasive argument. How am I supposed to push you away?"

"You're not." With only two blocks to go, he offered up one last reason. "The truth is I'm about seventy percent in love with you already. Are you really going to break my heart?"

CHAPTER SEVEN

HE'S SEVENTY PERCENT IN LOVE WITH ME?

The video feed from the garage camera blurred as Brenna tried to process that information. Fletcher's question about breaking his heart would be easy to laugh off if it had come from anyone other than him. None of the guys she'd dated had thought to check on her when she canceled a date or fought for her when she attempted to break up before the relationship got serious.

Are we enough of a couple to break up?

Considering the ache in her chest during the tough decision to distance herself from him, a resounding yes was the only possible answer. She'd also invited him to touch her intimately, which never happened before weeks or months of dating. Her actions this morning had been incredibly out of character for her.

She focused again on the camera feed at the flash of silvery blue on the screen. He was driving Laura's car again, which meant he'd made arrangements to borrow it to accommodate her needs.

He's thoughtful and considerate. And so damn sexy.

She didn't stand a chance in hell of resisting her attraction to him. "I'll do my best not to break your heart if you promise me the same thing."

"Done." His simple response came out quicker than she expected. "I promise. No breaking of hearts in our imperfect pancakes-and-bacon relationship. Are you meeting me at the door? Seems like a make-up kiss might be in order."

Surrendering to a giddy smile, she wheeled out of her office. "I'm not sure our discussion constituted a fight, but a hello kiss would be welcome. And then a happy-to-see-you kiss."

"Wow, two kisses. Seventy-five percent is probably more accurate."

She crossed the foyer and punched in the code to turn off the security system as the doorbell chimed through the house. The realization that she'd reached at least the fifty-percent mark didn't scare her, but the anticipation tickling her insides did. Charging into new situations wasn't in her DNA. She analyzed every minor decision and over-analyzed major ones, more so since her injury.

Falling in love was a major life event.

She smoothed her palms over her rebuttoned sundress, as nervous as she'd been at her first physical therapy appointment.

Just open the door. He isn't suggesting we get married today.

When she pushed on the handle and rolled backward enough to let him in, the concern etched in the lines near his eyes made her stomach flutter and her heart fall farther. If he proposed right this minute, she wouldn't have the brainpower to refuse.

No sooner did he close the door behind him than he leaned in and pressed his lips to hers. His fingers grazed her cheek and then he kissed her again. "Hi. I'm really happy to see you."

When he started to straighten, she clutched the front of his shirt to keep him within reach. "My turn. Hi. I'm happy to see you too."

After another pair of quick but tingle-inducing kisses, he eased away a few inches and grinned. "I like this much better than texts informing me you're canceling our date. Eighty percent."

"Same." At his surprised expression, she raised her chin, determined to own—and admit—her feelings. If he could, she could too. "On both counts."

He blinked at her, like he wasn't sure he believed her. "You don't have to—"

"I know I don't have to tell you I feel the same way you do, but it *is* true." She slipped her fingers through his and tugged him closer. "I like you more now than I did a week ago and yesterday and this morning. A lot more."

The look of adoration in his easy-to-read brown eyes warmed her insides. "We're all good now, right?"

She nodded, despite her lingering doubts about sex and orgasms. A single unsuccessful attempt wasn't the end of the world.

"Do you want to stay in or keep our plans to go to the concert in the park and have a picnic?" His tone didn't suggest a preference for one over the other. He was giving her the choice.

The sweetest by far.

Spending the late afternoon and evening away from her bed, her new vibrators, and the stress she'd put on herself would provide the break she needed. Being with this man while she cleared her head was a wonderful bonus. "I invited you on a date. Let's go out."

He seemed to suddenly relax, assuring her she'd made the right decision. "Okay. I was going to pick up some food at the grocery store to take with us. Do you mind if we swing by my house for a cooler and then stop for the drinks and stuff?"

"That sounds great. What are you planning to buy? Or is it a surprise?" She grinned up at him. "FYI, I like surprises."

"I remember. Then I won't tell you what Aunt Laura brought with her when she dropped off her car." His amusement changed to uncertainty. "Oh, but you were making dessert, weren't you?"

The heat of a blush crept up her neck. "I was too busy having a pity party when I didn't get a happy ending, not that I was going to actually bake anything. Dessert was supposed to be a euphemism."

A hint of pink shone through his tanned skin. "Yeah, well, we're going to have to hold off on the dessert you're talking about until I finish healing. The happy ending after I got home earlier led to taking a pain reliever and icing my lower abs and upper thigh."

"Ouch." She almost asked if she could kiss it and make it better, but that would probably exacerbate the problem. "We're quite the pair, aren't we?"

Still holding her hand, he crouched in front of her, not quite hiding a wince. "I think we're an awesome pair, and we'll get around to the euphemism kind of dessert eventually. No hurry."

"At least eighty-four percent." His bright smile added another point or two to the ever-increasing affection he inspired. Or maybe she'd already fallen in love with him. "Kiss me again."

He knelt in front of her and leaned forward, capturing her mouth with a tongue-tangling kiss. His fingers threaded into her hair, and he cradled her head as they continued the slow but thorough exploration. When he eased away, his panting breaths tickled her jaw. "Ninety-five or ninety-six."

A little short of breath herself, she giggled against his cheek. "Now you're just showing off, but I'm catching up."

With another of those tummy-tickling grins, he straightened. "I was thinking about bringing a blanket to sit on at the park. Or should I pick up a camp chair instead when I get the cooler? Whatever works for you is fine with me."

"The chair is fine. I don't want you to be in pain again from helping me onto the blanket. Back in about fifteen minutes. I'm going to make a bathroom stop and get my purse. Then we can head to the store." She flashed him what she hoped was a cheerful smile and wheeled down the hall toward her bedroom. Fifteen minutes was no exaggeration of how long the task usually took.

"Take your time." His trainers squeaked faintly on the wood floor as he followed. "I'll wait in the kitchen."

Wearing a dress helped shorten the time she needed, and she rolled up to the dining table where he sat thirteen minutes later, her disability placard in her lap. "Ready."

He shoved his phone in his pocket as he stood. "Me too. I made a list so I wouldn't forget anything. Lead the way."

Instead of hovering near the passenger door like he had when they'd gone to Lorenzo's, he popped open the trunk as she shifted to the seat. By the time he stowed her chair in the back and slid behind the steering wheel, she'd already buckled her seatbelt. The whole process reminded her of how easily her dad had adapted to chauffeuring her around town.

He frowned at her before he put the car in reverse. "I want to invite you into my house, but it doesn't have a ramp. Just steps at the front door and from the garage into the kitchen. I'm sorry. I'll be quick. Promise."

"No worries. It'll be quicker if you run inside by yourself

anyway." She reached over to reassure him with a gentle touch on the arm. "It's not your fault some places aren't accessible."

"But I want to be able to take you with me everywhere—without it being hard for you to get there." His softly spoken words toppled the remaining fifteen or sixteen percent in an instant.

She wanted to wrap him in a hug and never let go. "So we'll spend more time at my house than yours for now. And you can carry me once you're healed. Being held by you isn't exactly a hardship."

He tossed a crooked smirk her direction as he turned onto Main Street. "Easy for you to say. Hard is a state of being when I think about touching you. Maybe we should talk about something else, like the weather or who's playing at the concert."

The reaction between her thighs to his blunt honesty surprised her, but it also gave her hope that sexual satisfaction was still a possibility.

What if all I need is for him to be with me?

That was something to consider for later.

As it had during their pizza outing, conversation flowed easily during the short trip to his house and then to the grocery store. She'd hidden her feelings behind their work relationship, but now she had the freedom to express her attraction to him. Each touch, each shared gaze, each one of the smiles he aimed at her made her feel normal again—loved and necessary.

At the town square, he parked in one of the handful of disabled spaces near the bandstand, unbuckled, and rehung the placard from the rearview mirror. Then his lips met hers for a sweet kiss. "Thanks for asking me out. I'll be right there with your chair."

Not many people had arrived yet, leaving them plenty of room next to the sidewalk to set up their picnic. Her dad and Christy approached the gazebo from the other side of the block as Fletcher set his chair down next to the cooler.

Christy pointed toward them and waved.

Without missing a beat, her dad guided his wife toward them, his eyebrows scrunched downward to match his sudden frown. He leaned closer to her for a few seconds and then she shook her head.

When they stepped off the sidewalk, her dad stopped and braced his feet shoulder width apart, a pair of camp chairs hanging from his white-knuckled fist. "I didn't know you were coming, Bee. We could've given you a ride."

Christy flashed a narrowed-eyed glance at him. "Hi, Brenna. What your father meant to say is that it's good to see you here."

Brenna laughed at his stern expression. "Good to see you too, Dad. Fletcher, this is my dad and his wife, Christy. Christy. Dad. This is Fletcher Hayes, my date."

Despite the less than friendly look, Fletcher extended his hand. "Nice to meet you, Mr. Carlsen. Mrs. Carlsen. You're welcome to sit with us if you want to."

Christy's surreptitious thumbs-up at Brenna and approving grin were accompanied by an elbow to her father's ribs. "It's a pleasure to meet you too, Fletcher. Isn't it, Sven? And we'd love to join you."

He shook Fletcher's hand, but his glower didn't budge. "Fletcher Hayes. Are you related to Nate?"

With a nod, Fletcher withdrew his hand and laced fingers through Brenna's, sending warmth up her arm. "He's my uncle. I've been working for him since I moved back to Creekside in February of last year. Mostly framing and drywall. You have a roofing business, don't you?"

"Yes. I've done some work for Nate when he was short-handed, but I usually stick to my own roof and flashing repair jobs." Her father's jaw flexed. "How did you two meet?"

Fletcher winced. "She schooled me on hall and door widths when I wanted to cut costs for the accessible homes going in over at Creek's Edge, Uncle Nate's new project. I was on crutches at the time, so she proved her point pretty easily. And I apologized, of course. We went to school here in town together too. Graduated the same year."

"Hm." Her dad unfolded one of the chairs and gestured for Christy to sit. "Treat her right or you'll answer to— You'll answer to my daughter first and then me."

His last-second modification made Brenna snort. "Good save, Dad."

"I'm very aware of that, sir." Fletcher's mouth twitched, like he wanted to laugh, and he tipped up the lid on the cooler. "Would you like a water, Mr. Carlsen? Mrs. Carlsen? We brought more than we'll drink."

With a bit of unspoken encouragement in the form of a not-so-subtle nudge from Christy's foot, her scowling companion muttered a thank you and sat. He finally loosened up by the time the music started and managed a polite good-night when they parted at Laura's car at nine forty-five.

On the drive home, Brenna couldn't help but wonder if Fletcher's silence stemmed from her father's warning. "I'm sorry if my dad made you uncomfortable. He's overprotective of me. Always has been. I guess it goes with being my only parent. Even so, he shouldn't—"

"You don't owe me an apology. I get where he's coming from. You'll always be his little girl." He flipped on his turn signal as they neared her street. "Did you have fun tonight?"

"I did. Thanks for accepting my, um, bossy invitation." The stretches of darkness between the streetlights cast shadows over his handsome profile, but she caught the curve of his mouth in the faint light. Anticipation of a goodnight kiss and maybe something more set off wonderful tremors in her lower belly and between her thighs. "We didn't get to talk much, with all the people and music. Want to come in for a while?"

"Sure." He made the final turn into her driveway and shut off the engine. After leaning across the center console for a quick brush of his lips against hers, he retrieved her chair from the trunk. His muscles flexed as he unfolded it, positioned it at the passenger side, and locked the wheels. Then he double-checked the wheel locks and met her at the front door with his hands full. "I grabbed the last of the cookies and fruit in case we want a snack."

"Let's drop those off in the kitchen." She followed him inside, enjoying the view of his delectable butt in snug jeans as he walked down the hall. All the heat and desire from earlier had returned. Hopefully, he wouldn't leave before one of them did something about it.

CHAPTER EIGHT

"I NEVER WENT TO SEE A TRIBUTE BAND BEFORE. THEY WERE pretty good." Fletcher put the leftover strawberries and grapes in the fridge and then set the nearly empty cookie container on the table. "We should go to another one sometime."

Stopping beside him, Brenna reached for his hand. Her pulse sped up when he looked down at her with what she hoped was the same train of thought she had. The now-or-never feeling swirling in her chest urged her to seize the moment. "I'd like that. Right now, I'm thinking we could go make out for a while and maybe continue what we started this morning since we've had our first official date."

His eyes locked on hers, giving her a fair idea of how much he liked that idea. "Living room?"

She shook her head and turned toward the hall. "Bedroom. My new toys should be done charging."

The invitation was risky, but wasn't everything in life?

Footsteps trailed her to the master bedroom. His unsteady breathing suggested a bad case of nerves, much like her own. He stopped beside her at the bed. "Don't get me wrong. I want you—in every way. But I think I know how much figuring things out on your own means to you. Are you sure about this?"

She swallowed her fear of rejection and forged ahead. "I'm pretty sure I failed this morning because you weren't here. I was so turned on and that feeling faded when you left. Will you watch...and help? And talk to me. Tell me how much you want me and what you want to do with me when we're ready to take that step."

His face flushed, but the growing bulge behind his zipper at eye level encouraged her. He cleared his throat. "Like talk dirty to you?"

"There's nothing dirty about wanting to make someone feel good. They're just words." Embarrassment tried to flare up at the thought of him saying pussy or cock to her, but desire surged stronger still. She transferred from her chair to the bed and fiddled with the top button of her sundress. "Words that might make a difference."

"Okay." His lips covered hers as he sat and took over unfastening the front of her dress. The slow exploration of his tongue against hers stoked the fire he'd lit earlier back to life. Then he nibbled a path along her jaw to her ear. "I want to watch you touch yourself. Do you want to watch too? I can move the mirror so you can see us."

She nodded, despite hating the thought of not having his mouth on her skin for even a second. "Yes."

"Back in a minute." After another quick kiss, he retrieved the cheval mirror in the corner and positioned it by the cedar chest. "We can sit against the headboard once you're undressed."

He returned to his task, working his way down the long row of buttons from her breasts to her knees. Her blood hummed and her pulse beat in every cell by the time he finished, more so than this morning.

He seemed to rake his gaze over her body as he slipped the straps from her shoulders. Only her shapewear remained when he stood. "Perfection."

Her nipples tightened, and she tugged at the front of his button-down shirt. "Take this off and then sit against the pillows."

Not waiting for his response, she maneuvered to the middle of the bed and worked the stretchy shorts past her hips and off her legs. The weight of his intense watchfulness wasn't oppressive, feeling like curiosity instead of pity, and the half-expected yet completely dreaded offer of help never materialized.

He crawled into a spot across from the mirror and shifted a few inches to the right. The movement made his muscles flex and relax, drawing her attention. His crooked smile told her loud and clear that he'd noticed. "Which vibrator do you want?"

All in had been her motto on the endless road since her injury. Changing her attitude now was pointless. "Both of the rechargeables. May as well see if I like one better than the other."

Without losing his line of sight with his reflection, he retrieved the fully charged toys, set them on the covers next to him, and patted the space between his legs. "Ready to whisper not-so-sweet nothings in your ear."

She fought against the trembling in her upper body his husky promise triggered, using all her strength to move across the mattress to him. The warmth of his bare chest and stomach against her back calmed her nerves, but the press of his erection excited her.

He slid his bare feet under her ankles, raising their bare calves together with her knees hooked over his. Then his arms closed around her waist and his breath caressed her cheek. "Look at us in the mirror, Brenna. I can see your pretty pussy. Are you wet? Are you thinking about how good it's going to feel when you come? And that I'll be right here to watch it happen?"

Delicious shivers joined the needy ache between her thighs, compounded by the hunger radiating from his reflection. Her brain short-circuited, giving her no way to answer except with a nod.

He switched on the U-shaped vibrator and played with the settings on the remote control for a few seconds before handing it to her. "Simultaneous no-hands G-spot and clitoral stimulation. You can play with your breasts again too. I had that gorgeous image in my head when I jacked off in the shower this morning."

She whimpered, picturing his fist around his hard cock while water rained down over his naked body as she slipped the device into place. Tremors rippled through her with the first contact against her clit and G-spot.

"Now touch your tight nipples and watch in the mirror with me." He licked her ear lobe and released a rough exhale when she followed his instructions. "Fuck, that's so hot. So sexy. Are you trying to make me come in my shorts?"

His eyes met hers, amplifying the effect of his rumbly voice, his encouraging words, and the hum throughout her body.

He tapped on the remote, upping the vibrations and the overwhelming sensations racing everywhere. "Look at you, playing with your tits and fucking your pussy with your new toy. Are you close? I can't wait to watch you come so hard you scream. I want to eat your pussy next time. Taste every inch of you. Then I'm going to slide my cock inside you and fuck you until we can't move. Do you want me to—"

She cried out, swimming in the bliss surrounding her,

carrying her up and crashing down over and over again for what seemed like endless hours or days. The vibrations stopped, but the waves of utter satisfaction continued to ebb and flow as he groaned and jerked against her.

He tightened his hold on her and brushed his lips along her cheek, breathing almost as unsteadily as she was. "You are so…damn strong…and beautiful…and perfect."

The catch in his voice compelled her to turn toward him, to kiss and hold him too. "Will you stay with me?"

He eased their legs onto the bed and shifted until he was curved around her. "For as long as you'll let me."

Despite Brenna's slow, even breaths luring Fletcher back toward sleep, he eased his eyes open, hoping for a few minutes of watching her peaceful face while she slept. He hadn't planned to spend the entire night, but her invitation proved more powerful than his ability to say goodbye and go home alone.

Her lips tilted upward, although her eyelids didn't move. The dark halo of her hair rippled on the pillow when she tilted her head toward him. "You're still here. I'm glad."

Thrilled she hadn't expected him to make himself scarce by the time she woke, he pressed a kiss to the tip of her nose. "There's no place I'd rather be, especially when I'm a hundred percent in love with you."

Her slight smile widened as she blinked up at him. "That much, huh? What if I said I'm a hundred and one percent in love with you?"

He fought to speak past the sudden lump of emotion caught in his throat. "I'd be the luckiest guy in the world."

"I guess you're as lucky as I am then." She hooked her

arm around his neck and reeled him in for another kiss. "Can you stay for breakfast?"

"If you let me help." After one more quick touch of his lips to hers, he rolled to the edge of the bed to grab the towel he'd borrowed last night, casting a grin over his shoulder as he went. "No peeking. I'm going to get my clothes from the dryer."

Her playful laugh hit him smackdab in the heart. "Okay, I'll just look instead of peeking since you've already seen all of me there is to see."

He couldn't argue with her logic, but he wrapped the towel around his waist anyway and headed for the hallway. "I'll use the half bath so you can take your time in here. Meet me in the kitchen when you're done."

"I hope you like waffles."

"Love 'em!" The sound of rustling sheets almost made him go back, but he forced his feet to keep moving. She didn't need him to hover, like she wasn't capable of taking care of herself. She was, and he needed to remember that.

His first stop in laundry room unnecessarily reminded him of going off in his Jockeys last night during the most amazing orgasm he'd ever watched. Thankfully, the pressure of his shorts and her body against his groin had prevented another painful repercussion, and Brenna had seemed pretty damn pleased with the dual effect of her masturbation session.

He pulled his clean clothes from the dryer and carried them next door to the bathroom. Sleeping naked with her in his arms all night had been heaven, even though his dick had tried to convince him to slip under the sheet separating them. The slow approach to sex would give him the opportunity to work on other equally important parts of their relationship.

He wanted the whole deal with her—love, sex, marriage, family.

An image of them a few years down the road formed as he made coffee for himself and prepped the machine for a second cup for the woman he adored. Waking up next to her for the rest of his life was easy to imagine, as was making love with her, their wedding, and maybe a kid or two. He wanted to grow old with her.

The soft shoosh of wheels on the hardwood brought him back to the real world, and he pressed the button to start her coffee.

Her smile lit up the room when she rolled into the kitchen, now wearing a sleepshirt that revealed more than it covered. She stopped a few inches from him and inhaled. "This is why you get that extra one percent. I've never known anyone like you. Sweet. Kind. Thoughtful. Without thinking I need someone to do things for me. No, I take that back. Christy's always treated me the same way, but I don't want to date her."

The compliment made him glad for the conscious effort to stand back unless she asked for help. "Sometimes the urge to make things easier for you is pretty strong. I have to remind myself not to take over, that you were doing great on your own before I came along."

She threaded her fingers through his and gave his hand a light squeeze. "But I'm happier when I'm with you, and you're allowed to ask if I need help. I know it isn't out of pity. Oh, I just remembered something I've been meaning to do. Wait here. I'll be right back."

The gurgling and sucking noises from the Keurig covered the sound of her chair moving across the floor as she disappeared down the hall toward the foyer. He moved their mugs to the table and sat facing the way she'd gone.

Not much more than a minute passed before she reappeared through the living room doorway. Displaying her expert-level skills, she made a quick ninety-degree turn toward the kitchen and zipped along the wide corridor. "I found it!"

A hardcover book that looked familiar rested on her lap when she parked next to him. "Our high school yearbook?"

She opened it and started flipping pages. "Remember when I said my memory has holes?"

"Yeah. The accident. Severe concussion. In a coma for three weeks." She'd survived, a miracle he would never take for granted.

"I wanted to see if looking at your picture would spark a memory of you." She slowed at the first page of senior class pictures and skimmed her finger over the fourth row. Her sweet smile and bright blue eyes immediately caught his attention, even without her pointing out her portrait. "I can't believe it's been almost fifteen years since we graduated. The eight-by-ten is still on my dad's desk."

"Aunt Laura has mine hanging on the wall in the stairway. She and Uncle Nate never had kids of their own, so I basically had a second set of parents growing up. They've always treated me like I was their son too, especially after my mom and dad moved to New Mexico." He tapped on an action shot of him and his classmates installing runners for the door of the pole barn they were building. The hardhat hid most of his hair and face, but the duct tape holding his boots together and the giant rip in the back of his flannel shirt made identifying himself easy. "That's me on the ladder."

"Cute butt. That hasn't changed." She grinned at him and turn another page.

Grateful he didn't have a mouthful of coffee, he snorted. "So you want me for my body, huh?"

A mischievous giggle accompanied her shrug. "Well, it is a very nice butt. Fletcher Hayes. Second from the end of the row."

He cringed at the scrawny guy with a C-average GPA, social anxiety, and a drawer full of Sonic the Hedgehog t-shirts—the loser who should've gotten a least-likely-to-get-laid award. "As I mentioned, I'm older, wiser, and a lot less afraid to talk to you now."

Her finger landed right below his picture. She scrunched up her mouth and her eyebrows dipped low. "I think you helped me pick up a stack of papers. Flyers for freshman student council elections, maybe? They went slip-sliding all over the floor when I was hanging one outside the library. It was you, wasn't it?"

His pulse hiccupped. "You remember that? I thought I was going to have a panic attack when you said thanks and smiled at me."

"Is that why you ducked into the restroom without saying anything? I didn't know you were shy. Otherwise, I would've asked you to the fall dance instead of waiting for you to invite me." She looked up at him with the same mesmerizing eyes he'd fallen victim to in high school.

He laced his fingers with hers and leaned in for a kiss. "I think my chances with you are a lot better now."

"Your chances are very good. How are mine?"

"Excellent." He touched his lips to hers once, twice, three times before sitting back in his chair. "Ready to make breakfast?"

CHAPTER NINE

IN LOVE.

Brenna folded the last of her laundry, moved the stack of towels to her lap, and wheeled to the master bathroom linen cabinet. The task allowed her mind to wander, although it seemed stuck on Fletcher and her feelings for him. She'd been somewhat infatuated a few times in her life, but none of those brief relationships compared to the rightness of falling in love with him.

The images in the mirror were burned in her memory—the way he'd spread her powerless legs so she could touch herself, how his heated gaze had met and held hers, the look of elation on his face when her first orgasm in nearly ten years had pulled her over the edge into pure pleasure.

And he came from watching me.

Then he'd cradled her with his naked body all night, with no expectation of reciprocity, intercourse, or automatic permission to touch her in a sexual way. The sheet had remained between them in the darkness. His free hand hadn't strayed from hers, upholding his promise to let her set the pace for their physical relationship.

How could I not love him?

Her phone chimed in the side pocket of her chair, alerting her that her ride would arrive to pick her up in ten minutes. As she moved her cell to her purse, it buzzed in her hand and chirped with a text from her dad.

"On my way."

She sent him a thumbs-up and rolled to the kitchen for the container of peanut butter cookies she'd baked after Fletcher had gone home to shower and have lunch with his aunt and uncle. The time apart had dragged, even though her Sunday to-do list offered plenty of distractions. How would she survive until their date on Tuesday?

"Ugh." Shaking her head, she grabbed the cookies. "I'm stronger than that. I live by myself and have for most of the last ten years. Alone isn't the same as lonely."

Her phone chirped again. Her dad couldn't have arrived already, so she slipped it from the outer pocket.

"I miss you." A trio of red hearts popped up after Fletcher's message a few seconds later.

She bit her lower lip, but it didn't prevent her lips from curving upward.

"I can't wait to see you again."

The smile won, and her throat tightened. If he could show a little vulnerability, she could return the sweet favor. *"I miss you too. Can I call you later? About 8:30?"*

"Absolutely. Have a good time at your dad's. I love you."

Her heart fluttered, telling her everything she needed to know. *"I love you too."*

Then a smiley-face emoji with heart eyes appeared.

She surrendered to a full-blown grin and headed to the foyer. As she rolled outside to wait for her ride and reset the security system, her dad turned into the driveway in Christy's car.

He met her at the passenger side with a look she'd seen often during the earlier days of her recovery. "Hey, Bee. Any more problems with the roof?"

"Hi, Dad. Thanks for coming to get me." She lined up with the open door to transfer to the seat while he waited. "I haven't noticed anything."

"Good." His gruff tone was a sure sign he had something else on his mind, but he stayed silent until she'd settled in the car and he'd loaded her chair in the trunk.

When he finally slid behind the steering wheel, she took matters into her own hands. "What's bothering you?"

He glanced at her and huffed out a testy grunt. "Laura Hayes' car was here early this morning. The car Fletcher was driving last night."

She willed away the heat crawling across her cheeks and frowned at him. "And?"

His eyebrows dipped lower as he backed out of the drive. He clearly hadn't expected her to make him spell out the problem he had with her having an overnight guest. "Did you invite him to breakfast?"

Content to let him bumble his way through the questions he really wanted to ask, she turned her attention to her phone and ridding her email of its junk. "Yes."

"Oh." He cleared his throat and exhaled. "Did he... Did you... Never mind. I don't want to know."

Truly amused by his discomfort and awkward nosiness, she snickered. "Good, because it's none of your business."

He muttered something unintelligible under his breath, his jaw flexed, and his fists tightened on the steering wheel. Thankfully, he didn't say another word for the remaining six minutes of the drive or during the unloading process.

Christy met her at the front door with a quick hug. "Hi,

Brenna. I need your help with something. Sven, do you think it's time to uncover and preheat the grill?"

"You mean, make myself scarce so you two can talk? Sure. By the way, I love you more." He kissed her forehead and stalked away.

As soon as he was out of hearing range, she chuckled. "He's been out of sorts since he got back from an emergency repair this morning. You wouldn't happen to know why, would you?"

Brenna rolled her eyes. "He saw Fletcher's—his aunt's—car at my house, and he wants to know if my boyfriend stayed overnight, but he's too chicken to ask."

"Oh, that would definitely do it." Christy's support had almost convinced Brenna to call her Mom instead of using her given name numerous times over the last eight years. Her neutral stance and lack of judgment, however, made her more friend than parent. Even so, she played the part well. "If you want to talk about how the sexual aspect of your relationship is progressing, I'm glad to listen and offer feedback."

"Let's go get comfortable so we can chat eye to eye." Brenna led her into the living room and parked by the over-sized reading chair as her confidante sat. Ignoring the self-consciousness of the whole debacle, she shared the basic facts of Fletcher walking in on her while she was experimenting, the failure after he'd left, his return when she tried to cancel their date, and the subsequent success when he took her home. "We cuddled in bed afterward, and he spent the night. No pressure. No expectations. Just holding each other while we slept. Then we made breakfast together this morning. I've never felt more comfortable with anyone."

"I'm thrilled for you." Christy clasped her hand and gave it a squeeze.

Brenna let her emotions show in a smile. "He told me he

loves me, and I love him too. It's like nothing I've ever experienced. I know it's still early, but it feels right and as close to perfect as love gets."

"That's amazing. You deserve someone who sees *you*— smart, beautiful, kind, sensual—and not just a woman in a wheelchair. I know it doesn't seem like it sometimes, but your dad really does want you to thrive and be happy on your own. He's also the most protective man I've ever known." Amusement mixed with the affection in Christy's steady gaze. "Do you want me to talk to him?"

"Can we let him stew for a little while?"

Laughter echoed off the walls and Christy's follow-up smirk spoke volumes about her opinion. "It's your story to tell. You choose when."

Going with her gut, Brenna pushed past her ridiculous indecision. "So, I was wondering… Actually, I've been thinking about it for a long time. Is it okay if I call you Mom? I never had one and you've stepped into the position like it was a completely natural thing to do from day one."

"Oh." Her second biggest supporter leaned forward and wrapped her in a tight hug, sniffling through her words. "Yes. I'm so incredibly honored to have earned that title from you. Yes, yes, yes."

Tears wet Brenna's cheeks, reinforcing how important this connection was in her life, especially after growing up with only a biological mother who hadn't wanted any part of it. Then sobs let loose, bringing relief and joy and lightness to her soul.

"What happened? Do I need to have a talk with Fletcher?" Her father's panicked questions triggered teary laughter from Christy.

"They're happy tears, Sven." She hugged Brenna tighter. "She wants to call me Mom."

He sank to his knees beside them and wrapped his arms around them both. The firm yet gentle pressure brought back memories of her childhood, when he would remind her how happy he was to be her dad on a daily basis. His silence suggested he approved and couldn't find the words to say so without crying too.

At least a full minute passed before he loosened his hold. "You couldn't have picked a better one, Bee, and I'm lucky to have both of you."

Still blinking to clear her watery eyes, Brenna kissed his cheek. "We're lucky to have you. Oh, and Fletcher spent the—"

"No." He shook his head and stood, stumbling over his own feet in his rush. Then he marched out of the room. "Don't tell me. I'd rather be oblivious."

"He spent the night, and I swear we didn't have sex!" Maybe it wasn't the complete story, but she wanted him to like the man she loved.

"Argh!" His growly response carried down the hall, and what sounded like drawers and metal utensils banged and clanked for several seconds before the door to the patio thunked closed.

Christy collapsed into the chair, laughing so hard the tears kept flowing. "You know that only made it worse in his over-active imagination, don't you?"

Surrendering to a devious chuckle, Brenna nodded. "That was kind of the point. He needs to trust my judgment."

"He does." Christy swiped at her damp cheeks and sniffled. "Seriously. Without a doubt. He just doesn't trust any guy who wants to date you. It's so hard for him to accept that someone might break your heart and he can't do a thing to prevent it. You were his whole world for a lot of years, and he'll always want to fix whatever bad stuff happens."

On the verge of another sob fest, Brenna scrunched up her nose and grimaced to interject some more humor into their heartfelt discussion. "But, *Mom*, he has you to smother now."

"Why are you trying to make me cry again?" A huge grin accompanied another attempt to wipe away the nonstop tears. "Let's go see if your dad needs help with food and setting the table, *daughter*."

"Okay." Brenna trailed the most caring woman she'd ever known toward the kitchen.

I wish she and Dad would've reunited sooner.

Her father greeted Christy with a contented half smile and a kiss at the counter, proving that they'd found true happiness.

Christy directed the conversation through supper, mostly talking about ideas for this year's Claus for a Cause fundraiser and possible beneficiaries. The event had grown into a two-day festival since Brenna was the official recipient seven and a half years ago. Her matchmaking scheme between her father and his wife meant they were the official Santa and Mrs. Claus now, with the blessing of ninety-two-year-old Mrs. Barber, the original Mrs. C.

For once, envy didn't poke at Brenna's heart. The thought of Fletcher breaking it seemed ludicrous, considering his panicked concern yesterday morning when her front door had been unlocked and unarmed. That he'd dropped everything to convince her not to break their date wasn't the action of a man with temporary or calculated motivations. His easy will-ingness to accommodate her disability was something she seldom encountered, even among the few high school friends who still tried to include her from time to time.

He made every effort to accept her, imperfect as she was.

After making plans to have dinner again later in the week, she waved Christy in for a goodbye hug. "I love you, Mom."

"I love you too, Bee." Christy hugged her tighter for several seconds before letting go. "Talk to you soon."

On the drive home, her dad asked about an upcoming contract she'd mentioned in passing during supper, clearly trying to make up for letting his protective grumpiness get the best of him. "You've done a great job of building your business. I'm proud of you."

The same sense of accomplishment warmed her soul from the compliment he'd always been generous with. "Thanks. I learned a lot from you. You're the best dad."

"I don't know about the best, but I've tried to be a good father." He reached across the center console and clasped her hand in his. "I'm sorry for making you think I don't like Fletcher. He's a nice guy and you're a good judge of character. I should've kept my mouth shut."

She squeezed back, glad for the apology, even though she'd expected it. He never let disagreements simmer between them. "I know you worry about me, which I totally get. The thing is I think he's my person. You know, like you and Christy are for each other. I love him. He told me he loves me and I believe him. It feels right."

A hint of a smile appeared as he parked in front of the garage. "I'm happy for you. I mean it, and I hope he knows how lucky he is. He should come with you to sinner on Sunday so I can ask him."

CHAPTER TEN

FLETCHER SHUT DOWN HIS UNCLE'S LAPTOP AND STRETCHED his arms over his head. Desk duty was hell on his back, but at least he could move without risking a sharp pain in the groin today.

He pushed up from the chair, ready to go to the florist and the store to pick up a bouquet and a box of condoms and then drive to Brenna's for their date. The decision about whether to put a condom in his wallet or not had reached a standoff in his mind, despite the pros and cons running through his mind all day.

If he took one with him, did that make him prepared or hopeful?

A little of both was the honest answer.

What if he didn't, and she wanted to move to the next level?

I don't want to screw this up.

"Hey, Fletch, what's the frown about?" Uncle Nate strolled into the office, the coating of dust on his baseball cap, clothes, and boots announcing he'd spent the afternoon sanding drywall. "Muscles still bothering you? Laura said you were feeling almost back to normal today."

Fletcher shook his head. "I'm good. Just trying to make a decision before my date with Brenna."

Nate's right eyebrow rose and his lips flattened into a grim line. "If it's about carrying protection with you, the answer is yes, even if you don't plan on needing it. Behaving like a responsible adult is a no-brainer."

Heat seeped across Fletcher's cheeks, but he nodded. "I just don't want to rush things, you know? But being prepared is definitely better than being careless."

"Darn right, as much with women as on the job." His uncle leaned against the filing cabinet and straightened a second later, evidently deciding not to risk spreading the powdery dust everywhere. "You've been spending a lot of time with her. It's getting serious?"

"Yeah. She's pretty amazing, and I think she could be it for me. The one." The admission—saying the words aloud—brought a sense of calm instead of the hesitation and uncertainty his last relationship had sparked. "Being with her is so easy."

"Sounds like the real deal." After a quick pat on the shoulder, Uncle Nate waved toward the door. "Get going. You don't want to be late. Remember to invite her to the Fourth of July picnic on Thursday."

"I will, and thanks for the advice. See you tomorrow." Fletcher paused at his aunt's desk to say goodbye and then walked out the door, feeling more relaxed than he had in ages.

The oppressive oven in his truck meant driving with the windows down, but he refused to complain about the heat. He was in love with a woman who loved him back and his injury had finally healed enough to sneeze without doubling over in pain.

With a tissue-wrapped bundle of brightly colored flowers on the passenger seat, along with the box of condoms that had earned him a sly smirk from the college-aged cashier, he turned into Brenna's driveway at five twenty-nine. The garage door slowly opened as he approached, looking like an invitation to spend the night again.

She waited for him at the kitchen doorway when he pulled into the space and shut off the engine. Her bright smile amplified the desire to spend every minute with her. She rolled forward to the top of the ramp as he climbed out. "There's a chance of rain later. I thought you might appreciate parking inside."

To hell with it.

He grabbed the pharmacy bag with the flowers and hurried up the two steps to greet her with a kiss. "Absolutely. Hi. I missed you."

"Hi." She tugged him closer for another kiss, this one longer and more tempting than the first. Then she tapped the button on the wall beside her. "I missed you too. Come on inside."

The hum of the garage door closing faded when he followed her into the kitchen. He handed her the bouquet. "For you."

"Oh, thank you!" She closed her eyes and buried her nose in the overlapping petals. "They're beautiful. I love zinnias. What's in the bag?"

"I, uh… Something for later." He forced the words out of his mouth, even as his neck flamed and second guesses filled his brain. "In case we need it. Them."

Her lips curved into a wide grin. Then those gorgeous pools of blue looked up at him, drawing him deeper under her spell. "I might've had the same idea. Why don't you put them on the nightstand while I get a vase."

Tongue-tied and hoping his sudden hard-on didn't split his zipper, he carried the package to the master bedroom. The bedspread lay smooth over the mattress and a wrapped gift roughly the same size as the box in his hand rested against the pillow on the left. A nearly see-through midnight-blue nightgown was draped over the other.

All the blood in his body rushed to his dick. "Holy moly."

His fingers itched to touch the delicate lace almost as much as he wanted to touch her, but he forced his legs to move in the opposite direction.

Brenna shut off the water at the sink and set a tall vase on the counter. She swiveled toward him, the bouquet and a pair of curved scissors in her lap. "Can you grab the lettuce and cheese from the refrigerator? Hmm, it looks like you forgot to leave something in the bedroom."

He lifted the bag still in his grip and willed his brain to reset. "Oh. I got distracted."

The mischievous sparkle in her eyes and the tilt of her head were a clear admission of her intent. "What was so distracting?"

A few steps eliminated the space between them, and he feathered his fingertips up her bare arm to her shoulder. Only the narrow strap of her sundress stopped him. "Something lacy on your pillow. I can't wait for you to model it for me."

She gasped when he traced her collarbone to her throat. "Maybe we should do that now."

"Maybe so." He bent to nibble a path from her ear to her lips. A faint rumble came from his stomach, ruining the moment.

Her uninhibited laughter inspired his own. "That's a vote for supper."

Not giving him a chance to veto his grumbling belly's decision, she turned back to the sink and snipped off about an inch of stem from a zinnia. The end plunked against the stainless steel.

He sighed and kissed her forehead. "Another part of me would like to lodge a complaint, but it'll survive until later. Lettuce and cheese, right? Anything else we need from the fridge?"

"That's all for the moment." She placed the first trimmed flower in the vase and picked up another from her lap. "Any pain today?"

"Not so far. I'm hoping to be back out at the jobsite next week." The items he needed were in front on the top shelf, but something else caught his attention. "Is that homemade guacamole?"

A chuckle accompanied another snip and clunk. "You sound awfully hopeful."

"I am." He snagged what he needed and grinned over his shoulder at her. "I tried making it once, but the avocados were too hard to scoop out of the peel like the recipe said to do."

She laughed and shook her head. "The first rule of guacamole is to use ripe avocados. Very dark green. Almost black. And they should have some give to them. Not smooshy. Just a little soft. I can teach you next time I make it."

"I'm holding you to that offer, especially since it means I get to spend more time with you." He held up the block of cheese. "Grater? I know how to use one of those. Gotta have freshly grated parmesan for spaghetti, which I can make. With store-bought sauce."

"The drawer to the left of the stovetop." A trio of metallic thunks sounded and then she lowered more zinnias into the water. "If you want to expand your repertoire, I teach a cooking class at the community center once a month. I have to be careful to avoid upsetting my digestive system, so the menu includes recipes that are more likely to be safe for people with specific dietary needs. Don't feel like you have to, but I swear it's more than salad and tofu burgers."

"Sounds interesting. It's been just me cooking for myself since I moved away. I'm usually starving when I get home from work, and spaghetti, carry-out, and frozen pizzas are quick. Of course, it hasn't worked out so well lately. Three weeks of sitting at a desk all day and eating stuff like that has added at least five pounds to the scale." Instead of a metal stand-up version, the drawer contained a pair of flat graters with different-sized holes and a twirling kind servers used at restaurants. "Which of these should I use?"

"The bigger flat one. Black handle." A few feet away, she repositioned several flowers. Her gaze cut to his and held it. "I ate like that the same way a lot before the accident. Work eight hours. Spend an hour at the gym. Go home and eat whatever's easiest. I had to make a lot of adjustments when I came home from the hospital, besides the obvious. If you want some private lessons, I can arrange it."

He buried the urge to suggest he move in with her so they could cook every meal together. "Sounds even better. Grate some cheese. Earn a kiss. Chop the lettuce. Get another kiss."

She crooked her finger at him and wheeled backward across the room. "Ask for a kiss. Get more than you bargained for."

Curious about what she had in mind, he abandoned his task and joined her at the hall. The sultry look she aimed at him all but assured she wasn't talking about the tacos they were having for supper. "I love a good bargain. May I have a kiss?"

"When we get there." She tugged on the bow on the left

side of her dress before she set off toward the master bedroom. "Just so you know, it's a wraparound. No buttons this time."

At a loss for words again, he trailed after her. The subtle scent of her shampoo did little to settle his sudden case of nerves as he entered her private space. The lace nightie still teased him from its spot on her pillow, and the pale blue paper on the box hid nothing about its contents. It was the perfect setting with the perfect woman, but what if the experience was less than perfect for her?

She stopped next to the bed and reached for him. "Are you overthinking this as much as I was before you got here?"

"I'm guessing yes." He slipped his fingers through hers and sat on the mattress. "I want it to be amazing for you."

"I don't want you to worry about me. It might not be great the first time, but we'll be making love and that connection means so much more to me than any orgasm." Her confident expression was every bit as convincing as her words.

Speechless from her declaration, he could only brush a loose strand of hair from her cheek and savor the silkiness of her skin. Somehow, his feelings expanded to encompass his whole being—beyond anything he would've thought possible.

She guided his hand to the tie at her waist. "Are you ready for a kiss and more than you bargained for? I am."

He nodded and pulled at the narrow strip of cloth keeping her dress in place. The bow unraveled, allowing the overlapping pieces in the front to slump. Unable to resist, he peeled the fabric away from her chest to reveal one breast.

Her nipple puckered, and she let out a shaky breath. "Mouth first. Then you can kiss me anywhere my skin is showing. And you have to remove an article of clothing and let me do the same."

His dick went from interested to trying to bust out of his khakis from her invitation and offer of an equal trade. "I like this game. I get to choose where I kiss you?"

"If I can choose which item of yours comes off and where I kiss you." She blinked once as she hypnotized him with her blue-eyed stare.

"Of course." He leaned in and traced the seam of her lips, hoping to be welcomed inside.

Her tongue glided along his and slipped past his teeth. She explored and then lured him into her mouth by retreating. A soft hum vibrated through his jaw, making him wish he never had to break for air.

A second later, she eased away. Her cheeks were flushed and her breathing uneven. "I want to do that for hours, but I need you to kiss me other places too."

Faced with a major decision, he moved toward the most obvious spot rather than torturing them both by starting at her neck. After a gentle blow across her exposed nipple, he licked a circle around it and sucked the puckered tip between his lips. Her low groan encouraged him to flutter his tongue over the tight bud several times, earning him a gasp.

She whimpered when he released her. "My turn. Take off your shirt while I move to the bed."

He stood out of the way and fumbled with the row of buttons on his short-sleeved shirt, catching glimpses of her bare thighs as she got situated against the pillows, which didn't help his coordination at all. The shirt finally slid to the floor.

"Take off your shoes and socks too." She adjusted her dress to cover the same parts of her body it had before. "I wasn't wearing any, so they don't count."

His hiking shoes slipped off without fighting back, and he dropped his socks on the pile. "Anything else?"

Her small grin seemed like a sign she enjoyed being in charge. "Not yet. Sit next to me."

He'd no sooner joined her on the bed than she touched her mouth to his chest, imitating the licking, sucking, and tongue-flicking he'd done to her. A bolt of heat raced from his nipple to his balls, and a shudder coursed through his abs. "God, that feels good."

"Mm-hm." She sat up and untied a smaller bow at the inside seam of her dress. A few wiggles ended with both of her breasts bared, but more layers of flowered material covered her from about an inch below her belly button to her knees.

Not waiting for her go-ahead, he showered her other nipple with equal attention, drawing more sexy moans from her. He stripped his khakis off next and hoped he didn't embarrass himself again while she treated him to another round of foreplay. His cock responded to her duplicated treatment, grateful for the room to grow in his boxer briefs.

Instead of passing him the wrapped box of condoms, she folded back her loose dress, revealing a light pink pair of the shorts-like underwear she preferred. "Where are you going to kiss me now?"

Torn between exploring the smooth stretch of flesh from her ribs to her navel and nibbling a path from her fingertips to her shoulder, he shifted on the bed. Another idea formed in his mind. "Scooch down and roll onto your side, facing away from me. It's okay if I kiss your back, isn't it?"

She nodded and carried out his request. "I have some scars, but they don't hurt."

Several faint lines sparked an involuntary wince, but he gently kissed his way down her spine, focusing on bringing her pleasure and the freedom to touch every inch of her. Detours to her shoulder blades on the slow trek up again and nuzzles at her neck rewarded him with breathy sighs. "Have I told you I love you today? I do. A ridiculous amount."

"Mm. I love you too. A million percent." She turned her head toward him and kissed his jaw. "Underwear is next. Yours first."

"A million and one." After a peck on her cheek, he shed his boxers and tossed them over the side of the bed, unsure how the hell he would last more than two seconds when he was finally inside her.

"Sit against the pillows." She levered up on her elbow, a lusty smirk warning him of her plans.

He adjusted his position and bit his lower lip to attempt some control. "You know actual sex isn't going to happen this time if you do what I think you're going to, don't you?"

"I have every confidence in you." Her palm cupped his balls as she pressed a kiss to each one, forcing a groan from his throat. Then she traced the prominent vein along his length with her tongue in a barely there caress.

His hips tried to rise, but he forced them back down. "I'm about ready to—"

She closed her mouth around the head of his dick and swallowed at least two-thirds of him before he could protest —not that he would deny her anything. Light suction almost did him in.

Every muscle in his body shook as his eyes drifted closed and he let out a guttural moan. "Fuck. Fuck, fuck, fuck."

A muffled *pop* followed when she released him. "I want to do more of that later."

Spots danced in his vision and every hair on his body stood on end, like he'd gotten zapped by lightning. Dragging in a shaky breath, he fought to stay grounded. "Underwear off. My turn."

Her self-satisfied expression energized him enough to

grab for the box near his knee and tear off the wrapping paper. His hands stalled as he opened the end flap, his attention trapped by the sight of her shimmying the stretchy pale pink shorts past her thighs.

By the time he'd rolled on a condom, she lay completely naked beside him. "Don't forget to kiss me."

"No chance of that." He hooked his arms under her knees as he crawled between her gorgeous legs. The motion splayed her body open, giving him a closeup view of the image he'd seen in the mirror. "Tell me if you want me to stop—if it's too much or I'm hurting you."

She threaded her fingers into his hair and pulled him closer. "Kiss me, Fletcher. I'm so ready for this. For you. Love me."

Always.

He inhaled the mouthwatering scent of her arousal and pressed his lips to her inner thigh before moving on to lick a slow path through her folds. His tongue found her clit, but he circled it and headed back to her opening for a dip inside. A slight adjustment let him cradle her breasts in his palms as he found her sweet spot again.

Her desperate sounds urged him to stay, to tease her pussy and play with her nipples. "Right there. *Please.*"

Forgetting finesse, he alternately fluttered his tongue over her clit and sucked it into his mouth while he rolled her taut buds between his thumbs and fingers. Her abdominals trembled beneath his forearms, and rough panting blended with rising cries. He ignored the ache in his jaw, hoping to push her over the edge into pure bliss.

Her body shuddered and jerked against him at the same moment a high-pitched sob filled the room. The wild tremors and beautiful sounds of her release stole what little control he'd managed to keep hold of, and he guided himself inside her, gliding deep. Her muscles pulsed around him as he set an erratic rhythm, so close to joining her.

She tightened her grasp on his hair. "Faster. Harder. So good."

He dove deeper, letting sensations and emotions take over, determined to find immeasurable pleasure for and with her. Their voices echoed off the walls and in his mind as she gripped his cock tighter and freed him to join her this time.

The freefall seemed to go on forever, until he lowered himself on top of her, where he could once again kiss her forehead and nose and lips. In that perfect slice of heaven, one thought played over and over in his brain.

I want to spend the rest of my life with her.

CHAPTER ELEVEN

A CONTAINER OF ICED SUGAR COOKIES ON HER LAP, BRENNA wheeled toward the pavilion with Fletcher beside her. Attending the Hayes Builders' annual Independence Day picnic as a couple seemed like a big deal—an important statement about their relationship—since his family and friends would be attending.

The woman standing at what had to be the food table glanced their direction and hurried toward them. "Fletch, you're here! And, Brenna! I finally get to meet you in person. I'm so glad you could come. Are you two staying for the fireworks? Or are you going over to the high school parking lot?"

He greeted her with a smile. "We're planning to stay here. Less crowded. Brenna, this is my aunt Laura."

"Hi, Laura. It's nice to put a face to the name and voice." Genuinely happy to meet the friendly woman she'd spoken to on numerous occasions, Brenna smiled and held up the container. "Where should we put the cookies we brought?"

"I can take those while you go say hello to Nate. He can't wait to chat with you face to face about the project, even though work stuff is off limits today. My workaholic husband's over there firing up the grill." Laura pointed to the far corner of the structure.

"Thanks." After handing off her contribution to the picnic, Brenna led the way to Fletcher's uncle.

He looked up from adjusting the flames and grinned. "Brenna Carlsen. My favorite architect. The Creek's Edge designs are some of the best I've ever seen. I can't tell you how thrilled I am to be working with you. Any chance you might—"

Laura cut off whatever he'd been about to ask with a quick kiss on her husband's lips. "What did I say about leaving work at the office today?"

He chuckled, clearly amused by her intervention. "I can't help it if I'm a big fan of my nephew's girlfriend. What can we get you to drink, Brenna? A soft drink, iced tea, water?"

Brenna lifted her insulated bottle from the cupholder in her chair. "I'm all set for now. Thanks. If you want to talk business, we can meet for lunch one day next week."

"I'll check my schedule and call you tomorrow. Lunch is on me since I brought it up." His gaze darted over her head and he waved at someone behind her. "It looks like everybody decided to get here at the same time. I better put on my apron and start grilling."

The pavilion and surrounding grassy area filled with Hayes employees and their families. The overlapping conversations and laughter from the children playing on the nearby playground equipment unburied happy memories from her childhood. Fletcher's fellow crew members stopped for introductions and to ask when he would be back on the jobsite while he held her hand.

Her pulse hiccupped each time he glanced at her and

smiled. When he offered to hold the two-month-old baby belonging to one of the framers so he and his wife could finish eating, her ovaries practically had a meltdown.

Sitting next to him under the night sky with fireworks bursting above them, she let her mind ponder the possibility of marriage and children with him.

"Amazing, isn't it?" He leaned in, draped his arm around her shoulders, and pressed a feather-soft kiss to her temple. "I hope this never ends."

My heart is yours. Forever.

She snuggled closer, feeling treasured and loved and hopeful. "Me too."

What a way to start a Monday.

Despite having spent weeks in hospital-patient attire after the accident, Brenna flexed and relaxed her hands to keep from clutching fistfuls of the drafty medical gown. Regular doctor visits were part of her ongoing care, so she should've been used to them by now—or at least numb to the trauma her brain related to the smell of disinfectant and the nondescript examination rooms. She'd had at least a hundred appointments in the last eight years.

It's just a routine checkup.

Conjuring the adoration on Fletcher's face since they'd made love for the first time six days ago, she tried to calm her anxiety and slow her shallow breathing. A knock and then the click of the door opening snapped her out of the momentary peace.

Dr. Markwell stepped into the room, her white coat and the scrubs-clad nurse behind her adding to the irrational stress. "Hi, Brenna. Sorry to be running late. Early morning delivery. How have you been? Any problems or issues you want to discuss before the exam?"

"I've been doing well. Thanks. I have a list." Brenna picked up the phone from her lap and navigated to her notes. The words came into focus, but her fingers still tingled. "I should probably start with the fact that I became sexually active about a week ago. We're using condoms since I'm not on any kind of birth control, and I always go to the bathroom after to avoid the risk of a urinary tract infection."

"Excellent preventative care." Her gynecologist stood at the counter with her laptop, most likely making notes. "You mentioned wanting to talk to your occupational therapist about testing your body's responses last time we saw each other. Do you mind if I ask how things went with your partner? Did you have any pain during intercourse? Did you achieve orgasm?"

Willing away the heat creeping up her neck, Brenna cursed her embarrassment over a necessary medical conversation. "Christy and I made a plan and I was about to do some experimentation when my boyfriend and I started dating. I haven't experienced any pain, and I've had orgasms during foreplay and intercourse, which surprised me. It's been pretty mind-blowing, actually. I wasn't sure what to expect."

"That's really wonderful news." Dr. Markwell looked toward her with a broad smile. "What else is on your list?"

The next item was about annoyance and inconvenience rather than concern. Even so, Brenna forged ahead. "My period was a little heavier than usual last month. I know it isn't something I should worry about, but I'm used to it being predictable."

The doctor clacked on the keys, evidently adding that information to the file. "We'll see if anything seems off during the exam and go from there. Anything else?"

The final bullet point on her list tested Brenna's courage. She closed the app and inhaled, determined to know the answer, especially after seeing how much Fletcher had loved holding his co-worker's babies and playing with their kids. "The relationship I'm in... I feel like it's serious. I've done a bit of research myself, but I want your professional opinion. Do you think I can have children?"

Dr. Markwell's thoughtful expression as she looked up from the laptop gave Brenna no idea how she would respond. "You're my only patient with a spinal cord injury, so my experience is very limited. That said, I've attended talks and read studies about your condition to help me provide you with the best care I can. Women make up a relatively small percentage of SCI cases, but everything I've learned about your situation suggests fertility isn't affected by the injury once the body recovers from the trauma. Your menstrual cycle was back to normal about ten months after the accident. Based on that information, I'd have to say there's an average chance of conception for someone in your age range, meaning you're as likely to conceive as any other thirty-two-year-old woman with a healthy reproductive system."

Relief stole Brenna's voice for several long moments. "Thank you. I appreciate the extra effort you've made. I think those are all my questions for now."

With a nod, the doctor stood and gestured for the nurse to join her at the exam chair. "Feel free to call if you think of any others. We're going to lower your upper body all the way to the supine position and raise the leg support."

Breast exam, Pap smear, pelvic exam.

Brenna counted the dimples in the ceiling tile directly above her once the chair had shifted into a table and the checkup began. Narrowing her thoughts had become old habit with the endless hospital stays and appointments she'd endured. Dozens of physicians, technicians, and nurses had been part of her recovery. This checkup was a piece of cake compared to those.

"Hm." Dr. Markwell's pensive hum instantly broke Brenna's concentration. That sound was rarely a positive sign.

"What is it?" Immobile with her legs in the adaptive stirrups, she could only raise her head to look at the woman pressing on her lower belly.

Her doctor glanced up and then back toward the area she was manipulating. "I'm feeling a lump on your uterus. I'd like to do an ultrasound to see what we're dealing with. Possibly a small fibroid, which might explain the change in menstrual flow."

Forty minutes later, Brenna rolled onto the sidewalk in front of the medical building to wait for her ride, too overwhelmed to process her new diagnosis. It changed everything.

FRESHLY SHOWERED AND READY FOR A QUIET EVENING WITH the love of his life, Fletcher climbed in his truck. Traffic was light, even for a Monday, letting him make good time on the drive to Brenna's.

He turned into her driveway a minute early, shut off the engine, and grabbed the grocery bag with a few supper ingredients from the passenger seat. The front door swung open when he was halfway up the ramp.

She was watching for me.

The sight of her in the foyer sent his insides whirling and tumbling. "Hi. How was your day? I missed you."

Instead of looking up at him to accept a kiss, she moved away. "Can we talk?"

Her barely audible question stopped him in his tracks. His last girlfriend had said those exact words in that exact tone when she'd broken up with him.

No jumping to conclusions. This is Brenna.

He closed the door and tried to stop his pulse from pounding in his ears. "Sure."

She led him to the kitchen, but she wheeled to the patio door and faced the backyard rather than stopping at the table. "I need to tell you something."

A single thought popped into his head. He counted the days since they'd taken their relationship to the next level. Was a week long enough to know? "Are you pregnant? If you are, I'm right here for it. We'll get married if you want to. Or we can live together. Whatever works for you."

"No. Actually, I…" She dropped her head forward. "I had a doctor's appointment this morning. Gynecologist. Routine checkup. During the exam, she found something. An ultrasound shows I have several small uterine fibroids, and we talked about the effects and treatment options. They're not cancerous, but I may need to have them removed at some point, and there's a significant chance I'll have fertility issues because of where one of them is located."

Not cancerous.

The giant knot lodged in his throat eased as he dragged the closest chair next to her and dropped into it. She stiffened when he wrapped his hand around hers, but he didn't let go. "That must've been scary as hell. Are you okay? What can I do to help?"

Still more tense than he'd ever seen her, she swallowed loud enough for him to hear. "Fletcher, there's a good possibility I can't get pregnant. I know how much you want kids, so I think it's best if—"

"No." Disbelief put too much force into his reply, but how

could she believe he would choose being a father over her? "Listen to me. I can be happy without kids. I can't be happy without you. I love you and you love me. It's that simple. We can—"

The doorbell rang, and she pulled her hand free to retrieve her phone from its pocket. Then she whipped her chair in a tight half circle and propelled herself down the hall.

After the gentle thud of the door closing, a familiar voice carried toward him. "I'm sorry I couldn't get here sooner. Your dad wanted to know what's going on. Are you okay?"

Hissing whispers and a sob nearly ripped out his heart, followed by the quiet swish of wheels on the hardwood floor.

He caught sight of Brenna as she disappeared down the hall with her visitor not far behind.

Mrs. Carlsen walked toward him after a brief hesitation. Her gaze locked on his at the entrance to the kitchen and stayed there as she crossed the room. "I'm guessing she told you about what the doctor found this morning and decided the best way to protect you is to push you away."

On the verge of breaking down himself, he nodded.

"I get that it's easier said than done, but give her a few days to process her diagnosis. She's been through so much and has the first-born only-child tendency to forget that she's allowed to rely on the people who love her. To hear Sven tell it, she's been stubbornly independent since the day she was born." Wrapping her arms around him, she pulled him into a slightly comforting hug. When she released him, a stern expression replaced her sympathetic one. "I know it's hard to step away when things have been going so well. I promise this is just a bump in the road. No matter what, don't give up on her."

As much as he wanted to swear he wouldn't accept defeat, doubts rumbled in his brain. "What if—"

"She loves you, Fletcher. Trust in that." She clasped his hand and walked with him to his truck. "I'm going to go check on her. You'll both be okay. Drive safely."

Without another word, she hurried inside.

The closed door left him feeling completely lost.

CHAPTER TWELVE

BRENNA CLOSED HER EYES AND MASSAGED HER TEMPLES, in hopes of easing the tension headache crawling through her neck and shoulders. The lone positive that had come from four days of research was confirmation of Dr. Markwell's assurance uterine fibroids weren't cancerous. They did, however, tend to grow over time and cause infertility in some cases.

I made the right decision.

Her heart and soul ached, but Fletcher deserved better than what she could give him.

Keep telling yourself that. Maybe you'll believe it in fifty or sixty years.

Tired of fighting with her conscience, she scrolled through the remainder of the week's tasks and appointments, hoping for something to distract her for another half hour. Other than a virtual meeting with her team tomorrow morning, her work was essentially done. Putting in twelve hours a day since Monday meant she'd jumped ahead of schedule.

Her phone buzzed next to the keyboard, yanking her

attention from her calendar. Christy's name shone on the screen.

"Pencil me in for lunch on Saturday at noon. Your house. My treat. We haven't done our monthly assessment yet and it's already the 11th. Hungry for anything specific?"

"Ugh. Food." Her appetite had deserted her, but skipping meals and eating junk messed with her digestive system and bathroom schedule.

She picked up her phone and sighed. *"Salad from Maxwell's Diner. With fruit and goat cheese."*

A thumbs-up appeared in the conversation. *"See you then. Love you."*

Tears stung her eyes from the simple sentiment. *"Love you too, Mom."*

Why had she waited so long to recognize her dad's wife as her mother? Christy had been her ride-or-die protector and friend since the night they'd met.

She added a red heart, even though hers was broken.

SLAPPING ON ANOTHER TROWEL OF DRYWALL MUD, FLETCHER filled in the dent he'd sanded into what should've been the final coat. His concentration was shot to hell and he was bleeding out.

The echo of boots on the underlayment warned him Uncle Nate had stopped to check on his progress. "What did that wall ever do to you?"

Instead of answering, Fletcher grunted.

A heavy hand landed on his shoulder. "It was breaktime an hour ago. Go grab a sandwich and something to drink. That's an order."

"Not hungry." His stomach growled, arguing the point. "I'll eat in a minute. I just need to finish—"

"Now." His uncle snagged the trowel from his grip and set it on the overturned bucket. "Or I can put you back on desk duty. That'll give you lots of time to think about how unfair life is sometimes."

"Unfair? Are you fucking kidding me?" Fletcher stomped across the future living room, sat his ass on the step stool, and shoved his fingers through his hair. "Unfair is a bad call in a baseball game. Or getting a ticket for going two miles per hour over the speed limit. I should be with Brenna, supporting her and making sure she knows how much I love her."

"Maybe unfair isn't the right word, but you're letting what's going on in your personal life spill over into the job. I need to know every member of my crew is safe and doing their best. You can't do that if your mind is somewhere else." The steady scrape of the mudding knife in Uncle Nate's grip was a reminder that he could fill in for anybody anytime. "Have you heard from the Carlsens?"

His frustration now tempered by exhaustion, Fletcher rested his elbows on his knees. "Mrs. Carlsen texted me last night. The doctor wants to check Brenna in six weeks to see if there's any change. Maybe surgery after that. I don't think I can wait months for her to let me back into her life, but what choice do I have? I'm stuck in this dark place without her."

"Okay. What do you want to do about it?" More scraping accompanied the question. "Let me rephrase that. If nothing was off-limits, what would you do?"

The answer was simple. "I'd ask her to marry me. Tell her she's the most important person in the world to me and I want to spend my life making her as happy as she makes me."

"Then what's stopping you?"

A million reasons filtered through his mind, but only one truly mattered. "The chance that she'll say no."

"And if you're sure she's doing it to protect you? What will you do?"

Again, the answer was simple—simpler than it had been five minutes ago. "Tell her I'd rather protect her and I'm going to ask her until she says yes."

His uncle lowered the trowel into the bucket of water and wiped his hands on the towel draped on the ladder. "Problem solved. Go eat."

§

A WEEK HAD PASSED SINCE FLETCHER HAD PROMISED TO BE patient for a few days while the love of his life worked through her feelings and her misplaced self-sacrifice. Kids weren't a dealbreaker, not that he and Brenna didn't have other options if infertility was a problem they couldn't overcome.

Mrs. Carlsen—Christy—had finally agreed to intervene after two more updates of no progress with the most stubborn person she'd ever known. She and Brenna had plans to meet at Lorenzo's at six for comfort food and time away from work.

He rubbed the towel through his wet hair, wiped a spot to clear the mirror, and then tossed it over the shower door. The man staring back at him looked tired and in need of a haircut. Finger-combing didn't help, so he swiped on deodorant and headed into the bedroom to dress.

His hyped-up nerves pushed him toward wearing khakis, a dress shirt, and tie, but common sense told him office clothes wouldn't impress her. Instead, he opted for a button-down shirt and his nicest pair of shorts paired with his mostly clean hiking shoes.

Phone, wallet, keys.

Last, he picked up the velvet box from the top of his dresser and inspected its contents. The diamonds sparkled in the light through the blinds, despite their modest size. It was the best he could do, considering the other purchase he'd made today and would take ownership of tomorrow.

Let's do this.

Stuffing the tiny box in his pocket, he walked out of his room, doing his best to stay calm. If she refused his proposal, he would try again. The long haul was his objective, and she would eventually realize he wasn't going anywhere.

At least that's the plan.

His gaze skipped to the digital clock on the dashboard at each stop sign and traffic light, like his eyes had a mind of their own. The numbers switched to seven fifteen as he flipped on his signal three driveways from Brenna's house.

Christy's car approached from the opposite direction and made the turn ahead of him. He parked beside her in front of the garage, leaving plenty of room for her companion and the wheelchair.

When she climbed out, he did the same, meeting her at the trunk. Her slight frown didn't bode well. "She knew it was a setup as soon as she saw your truck. You have three minutes. She's already upset."

His chest tightened, as much from guilt as misery. "Okay."

Unwilling to waste a second, he rushed to the passenger door and knocked on the window. The indifferent stare that greeted him warned him of an uphill battle.

He dug the ring box from his pocket and forged ahead anyway. The ring caught rays from the setting sun when he flipped up the lid to show it to her. "Will you marry me, Brenna? I'm here for better or worse. In sickness and in health. For all of it."

She shook her head, and a tear streaked down her cheek.

More than anything, he wanted to hold and comfort her. "Brenna, do you love me? Do you believe I love you?"

Glancing toward her lap, she ignored his question.

"Unless you can honestly say you don't love me, I'll be waiting for you for as long as it takes. I'm not giving up on us, and I'm going to ask you every day until you're ready to say yes." He willed her to look at him, but she hid behind the fall of her silky hair. Taking that as his cue to leave, he tucked the ring in his pocket for safekeeping. "I love you, Brenna."

His body and soul hurt from the lack of acknowledgment as he slid behind the steering wheel and drove home. Thankfully, tomorrow offered him another chance.

ARMED WITH AN INSULATED MUG OF ICED COFFEE—THE caffeinated kind—and the bottle of acetaminophen, Brenna wheeled past the kitchen table with the vase of red, pink, and white roses that had been delivered yesterday at lunchtime. A handwritten proposal had accompanied the bouquet, setting off another round of tears.

She was almost situated at her desk when the doorbell rang. The app on her phone showed a young man descending the stairs and a book-shaped package sticking out of her mailbox.

Backtracking to the hall took more effort than usual, tempting her to leave the delivery where it was and go take a nap. If not for the virtual appointment she'd made with Dr. Markwell in less than twenty minutes, she would have.

With the box on her lap, she returned to her office. A mix of dread and curiosity convinced her to cut through the packing tape and unwind the bubble wrap from whatever was inside. An envelope slipped free as she finally uncovered a simple wood frame. The photo triggered more tears from the seemingly endless supply she'd had since ending her relationship with Fletcher.

She brushed her fingertips over the enlarged photograph that must've been taken by Laura or Nate at the picnic. Fletcher's smile and the pure adoration he aimed at her as she grinned back at him let a sob break through. He'd spoken the truth when he'd proposed to her.

He loved her, and he wouldn't give up on their happily-ever-after, no matter how long he had to wait.

It was right there on his face for everyone to see.

But he only cares that I see it.

After a mostly ineffective swipe at the wetness on her cheeks, she opened the card. "Will you marry me?" was scrawled across the front on a background of pink and red hearts, and most of the white space inside was line after line of his blocky writing.

"Dear Brenna,

I miss you every second of every day that we're apart. Someday soon I hope you'll say yes so we can share our lives and our future. You're the strongest person I've ever known, but I'll always be here if you need to lean on me. I know you'll do the same when I need you.

You're the reason I want to marry you. Just you. I can't imagine loving anyone else like this. Making you happy and putting a smile on your beautiful face is the best thing I could do with my life. If having a child does that for you, I'll make it happen. We'll find a way.

We can do this together.

Love always,
Fletcher

How was she supposed to say no to his soul-bearing honesty?

She tugged several tissues from the box near her monitor to wipe away the tears, but the probable splotchiness from crying was a lost cause. Hoping the iced coffee would unstuff her nose and boost her energy for the consultation about to start, she took a long drink.

Her phone buzzed and lit up with a text message containing a link to join the video chat as she stood the framed photo and card in the only empty spot on her desk.

A click connected her with Dr. Markwell. "Hi, Brenna. I understand you have some questions and concerns. Tell me what's going on first. Are you having any of the symptoms we talked about?"

Glad to get straight to the discussion, Brenna navigated to her list. "I'm not sure. I've been really tired the past few days, but my boyfriend and I... I broke up with him, so I haven't been sleeping well. And I've been feeling pretty emotional."

"Of course. I'm sorry to hear that. You seemed excited about your relationship and exploring the sexual aspect of it." A faint sound, like typing, joined her doctor's voice partway through her statement.

Focusing on her list, Brenna moved to the next item. "I haven't had any cramps or abdominal pain, but my breasts are tender. My bras feel uncomfortable and I have to be careful how I lay in bed."

"Hm."

"Is that a good hm or a bad hm?" Thinking back to her previous appointment, Brenna braced for the worst.

"I'm not sure yet. When was the first day of your last period?"

A search of the calendar on her laptop yielded the answer. "June fifteenth. It was a little heavier than usual, like I mentioned before, and it lasted five days."

"So, four and a half weeks ago, correct?"

"Yes." Brenna barely refrained from groaning. Irregular periods would mean a complication she didn't need. "It's been twenty-nine days for about seven years. Could the fibroids be messing up my schedule?"

"Possibly, but I suspect something else is causing the change. Are you available to come in for a urine test today? Drop-in is fine, and I can take a minute to discuss the results with you in between patients."

Abandoning her list, Brenna moved back to the video chat. "What are we testing for?"

Dr. Markwell paused her note-taking. "I think there's a chance you may be pregnant."

Brenna blinked at the woman on her phone. "But you said the fibroids… Pregnant? Are you sure?"

"Your symptoms suggest you could be. We'll know more after the test." Her doctor glanced away and then nodded. "I need to go, but we'll talk more after we have the results. See you soon."

"Yes. Okay. Thank you." Still a bit stunned, Brenna set down her phone and tried to focus on filling her lungs so she wouldn't pass out.

How was it even possible?

Fletcher had used a condom every time, and neither of them had noticed a failure.

Another gulp of coffee helped her brain reset, at least enough to think about next steps.

She dialed Christy's number, even though she was likely at work. When her voicemail picked up, Brenna left a message to call her back as soon as possible.

Eight endless minutes later, Christy's name lit up the screen. "Mom, do you have time to go with me to the doctor's office today?"

Controlled panic laced her mother's voice. "What's wrong? Do I need to call your dad?"

"No." Brenna closed her eyes and sighed. "Dr. Markwell wants me to come in for a pregnancy test."

"Oh. Wow. Okay." Christy sounded almost as shocked as Brenna had felt. "I have clients all morning and I'm doing a training this afternoon. So, um, maybe you should ask Fletcher to go with you."

THE SILENCE WAS GOING TO SEND HIM OFF THE DEEP END.

Fletcher rubbed his palm over the final powdery strip of sanded mud, determined to ignore the what-ifs running laps in his head. The smooth surface brought relief and no satisfaction. His job was safe for now, not that working with the crew was better for his attitude than sitting in the office.

He stalked out of the soon-to-be kitchen for a breather and a water break. The wall of humidity as he left through the garage was almost worse than the mask he'd worn for the last hour. Sweat had already soaked his t-shirt, inviting him to dump a water bottle over his head and grab a second one from the cooler to drink.

His parched mouth won, and he drained half of the contents before resurfacing for a breath. A bead of sweat evaded the bandana on his forehead, traveling along his hairline to his jaw. He pulled the hem of his shirt upward to swipe it away at the same time his cell vibrated against his leg. Glad for a distraction, he pulled it free. Dread and hope join forces when he saw Brenna's name.

"I need to go to the doctor's office. Do you have time to go with me today?"

His stomach dropped to his knees, but he jogged to his truck instead of waiting for it to recover. *"Are you hurt? I can be there in ten minutes."*

"Not an emergency. It's just a test I need to have done."

The sudden urgency stalled him with the door handle in his fist.

"Where's the fire?" Uncle Nate grasped him by the arm.

"Brenna needs me." Fletcher fought to calm the adrenaline pushing him to hurry. His fingers shook as he typed in his response. *"I can still be there in ten minutes."*

Dots appeared and disappeared several times before her message landed in the conversation. *"Okay."*

His muscles let go of some of the tension, and he could almost breathe again. "I thought something was wrong, but she was just asking if I could go with her to have a test done at the doctor's office. Something routine, I think. She's finally ready to see me. I can't say no."

"Go." His uncle gave his shoulder a firm squeeze. "Let me know when you're heading back or if you need to take the rest of the day off. Be careful."

Grateful for the understanding, Fletcher gave a quick nod before he climbed into his truck. A quick stop at his house cut into the seconds ticking off his ten minutes, but switching vehicles and retrieving the ring were necessary tasks. He arrived in her driveway as the clock on the dash counted down to zero.

She crossed the front door's threshold as he shut off the engine. Not waiting for an invitation, he met her at the bottom of the ramp.

Her eyes were red-rimmed and her cheeks were flushed, like she'd been crying. "Hi. Thanks for going with me."

Fighting the urge to wrap his arms around her and hold her forever, he stuffed his hands in his pockets. "No problem. All you have to do is ask and I'm here. Are you ready to go?"

"Yes." At his gesture to take the lead, she wheeled to the passenger side. "You were at work. Did you have to borrow someone else's car?"

He opened the door and stood aside so she could get into position. "It's mine. I bought it a couple days ago so I wouldn't have to keep borrowing Aunt Laura's."

She froze with her hands prepared to move from her chair to the seat. "You bought a car? Because of me?"

He shrugged, hoping she didn't change her mind. "I should have a vehicle you can get in and out of."

With her lips pressed together in a thin line, she expertly lifted herself into his new-to-him sedan.

As soon as she was buckled in, he stowed her chair in the trunk—the one he'd measured four times to be sure it was big enough. The ring box in his pocket bounced against his thigh with every step to the driver's side and again when he sat behind the steering wheel, testing his patience. "Where are we going?"

"The medical building next to the hospital." She glanced toward him as he shifted to look out the rear window. "Dr. Markwell's office."

Worry attacked his gut for the millionth time, but he refused to add to hers. "I looked up uterine fibroids. What kind of test is she doing?"

A full block passed with only the sound of the AC.

Her hair fluttered in the cool air blowing from the vents, and she tucked it behind her ear. "A urine test."

"Why? Does she think you're misusing pain medication or something?" He flipped on his turn signal and kept his attention on the upcoming traffic light.

"No, nothing like that. It's…" She shook her head. "Let's wait until we're there."

Every worst-case scenario flooded his thoughts. Could a urine test tell if someone was dying?

Three more blocks slogged by while his imagination went on a frightening ride. The light went from red to green as he finally approached the entrance to the parking lot. He aimed for the closest empty spot, leaving a longer walk than if he'd been willing to wait a little longer.

Muscle memory took over as he unloaded her chair and rolled it to her door.

Please let her be okay.

Setting one dusty boot in front of the other, he walked with her to an office located several yards beyond the first-floor elevators. Several people sat in the waiting area, not that he could've said how many or what they looked like.

A few minutes later, he sat in an exam room by himself while Brenna trailed after a nurse to the restroom. His knee bounced up and down for the count of eight hundred before he switched legs and started over. Then he paced the ten-by-twelve space until footsteps announced someone's presence in the hallway.

The door swung inward as he sat, and Brenna entered alone. "Dr. Markwell will be in with the results soon."

"Okay." He sucked in a shaky breath and tried to prepare himself for bad news.

She reached for him, lacing her fingers through his when he lifted his hand to hers. The feel of her skin soothed some of his nervousness. "I'm so sorry for pushing you away, Fletcher. I love you and I know you love me. I just wanted everything to be perfect for you. If you'll still have me, will you marry me? And thank you for the gifts. The picture is perfect."

His heart nearly stopped. "You're not dying, are you? What was the test for?"

"No, I'm not dying." She tightened her hold on him. "I need you to answer my question before we talk about the test. Will you marry me?"

"Yes." The oppressive weight that had threatened to smother him lightened. He worked the box out of his pocket and handed it to her. "I wouldn't have asked you if I wasn't serious. This is yours, and you're not ever allowed to give it back."

Her genuine smile chased away the ache he'd been carrying around for ages. "The test is to see if I'm pregnant."

The room swayed as her words sank in. "I thought you couldn't... But... Pregnant? Are you sure?"

Her lips parted, like she was about to speak, but a trio of quick raps on the door interrupted her.

A woman in a lab coat entered, her unreadable expression hiding what he needed to know. She nudged a backless chair out from under a low counter, sat, and extended her hand toward him. "I'm Dr. Markwell. Am I correct in assuming this is your partner, Brenna?"

Brenna nodded at the same time he shook the doctor's hand and introduced himself.

"It's nice to meet you, Fletcher." The doctor grinned in Brenna's direction and shook her head. "You continue to defy the odds, young lady. The urine test confirmed what I suspected during our chat earlier. Based on the date of your last period, you're about two or three weeks along."

Only half listening to her rundown of immediate care changes, he leaned in to give Brenna a kiss and a lingering hug. "How soon can we get married?"

EPILOGUE

FLETCHER FIDDLED WITH THE PLATINUM BAND IN HIS POCKET, rubbing his thumb over the imbedded stones, as Mr. Carlsen opened the patio doors and smirked at something his wife whispered in his ear. They walked outside and sat with Aunt Laura and Uncle Nate, his parents, and Brenna's grandparents on the two white benches. Standing between him and their families was Creekside's mayor.

The traditional wedding music they'd chosen barely registered when his vision in white rolled into view. Airy fabric floated around Brenna's legs and draped in soft folds over her torso, in a more delicate version of the sundresses she liked to wear. Her eyes met his, sending his pulse into a faster rhythm and bringing his whole world into focus. Happiness lit up her face, and she shared her joy with him. Their life together had already begun, but today's ceremony was for everyone else to witness their commitment.

She stopped in front of him, immediately reaching for him and renewing the physical connection they couldn't seem to get enough of. After a glance at the mayor, she looked up at him with a breathtaking smile. "I, Brenna Carlsen, do take you, Fletcher Hayes, as my husband, my partner, and my soulmate. You are the love of my life and the center of everything to me. We'll experience ups and downs, but I'll be here to support you and I know you'll always be here for me. I cherish every moment I get to spend with you, and I can't wait to see what our future holds. I love you with all my heart. The ring I give you is my promise to put you and that love above all else."

His throat tightened as she slipped the polished band onto his finger, and he had to swallow hard to offer his own vows. "I, Fletcher Hayes, do take you, Brenna Carlsen, as my wife, my partner, and my soulmate. My heart is full with you beside me, and my world is so much better because you're in it. I'm thankful for every day we have together, even if we sometimes have imperfect days. They make us stronger and remind us to rely on each other. I love you for always. The ring I give you is my promise to put you and that love above all else."

He eased the diamond-studded ring onto her finger and bent to touch his lips to the back of her hand.

The mayor sniffled and covered their hands with her own. "Fletcher and Brenna, inasmuch as you have declared your intention to wed and have exchanged vows and rings, I now pronounce you husband and wife."

Not waiting for the prompt, he met Brenna halfway for a kiss. "And they lived happily-ever-after."

Have you read Sven and Christy's story? Available now!

ABOUT THE AUTHOR

Mellanie Szereto is the *USA Today* Bestselling Author of over sixty romcoms and contemporary romances, most with characters who have plenty of life experience like herself. Whether you call them older, seasoned, mature, experienced, or later-in-life protagonists, they deserve love too! Her stories are often set in small towns with quirky main characters, fun secondary casts, and lots of humor. She enjoys gardening, cooking, and baking—as well as hiking to work off the fruits of her labor—and incorporates food into all of her stories. She lives in an old farmhouse in rural Indiana with her husband of thirty-eight years.

Visit her website for more information about her books!